READ N

C

The Leather Bottle
A short story set in Kansas City

She was determined to give him a birthday celebration he definitely would *not* forget – even though she might be putting their long happy thirty year marriage at stake. She – Clare - was driving, as usual, so that John could enjoy the journey without the hassle of the amount of traffic at this time of day. It was only a short drive to the restaurant.

"There's a good spot to park over there, not far from the entrance." John was pointing to the empty bay close to where diners were just starting to file into the restaurant. The doors had just opened.

Clare made sure they left early enough to find one of the 'Disabled' bays still free. They were in luck. John, her husband, was still able to walk pretty well – on one of his 'good days' – but recently his Alzheimer's was becoming less predictable. Over the past five years during which it seemed he was slowly retreating into a hibernation, she had learnt to keep things as simple as possible. This included booking a quiet window table for the few occasions she was brave enough to treat them to lunch out and, of course, finding a convenient place to park.

Clare checked her hair and make-up in the rear view mirror before getting out of their red sports convertible, making sure she got to the passenger side before John started to struggle with the door handle.

Although I won't see sixty again, there's no excuse to let standards drop, she thought as she smoothed down her skirt.

"Where are we going?" he asked, the usual puzzled look clouding his face.

"Where we said we would. The Leather Bottle. The restaurant. It's the first day of spring and your seventy fifth birthday."

John said nothing. At least he was rarely argumentative these days, given his condition. Just confused. Today *was* a good day and he took Clare's helping hand without complaint as he stepped out of the car. She ran her hand – lovingly – over the front of his hair line, temporarily 'dislodged' by the gentle spring breeze as they drove the two miles from home in their open-top coupe.

They joined the queue, such as it was – thankfully just a handful of people (John didn't like crowds). It ended at the point where the head waiter greeted the diners before allocating them to reserved tables.

"Do you have a reservation, sir?"

"What?" answered John, too quick for Clare this time.

"Yes," she replied, saving John's embarrassment, "a table for two. Name of Sercombe. By the window."

"This way madam," said the waiter, leading them both – John behind, then Clare. "Table for two, by the window. I'll fetch the menus." There were four chairs.

"Is someone else coming?" he asked.

Clare panicked for just one brief moment, fearing he had guessed her surprise, before realising 'how could he?' She decided to ignore the question, hoping to get away with it this time. That didn't always work. Sometimes it irritated John even more than if she gave him an answer he didn't like.

Instead, Clare saw to it that John was comfortably seated in one of them, facing the garden and away from the other diners. The serenity of the garden would give him peace of mind. Kee him calm. And avoid the risk of him making comments – not always flattering – about the other diners. She poured him a glass of water before taking her own seat.

The menus arrived.

Lunch was ordered, delivered, despatched and the plates cleared without incident – and at a pace that suited John well. If the service was too slick, John felt rushed and unsettled; too slack, and he fidgeted and played with the cutlery and condiments for amusement.

'This IS a good day,' Clare said to herself, but she still wasn't sure how John would react to her special surprise. Even as they left the house she was having second thoughts. *'Had she done the right thing? He was used to routine, everything in order, all things in their place.'* This meant people as well as things. *'How would he react?'* she wondered.

Also, his memory had become worse in the past few years. *'Would he remember? And, even if he did, would he recall all that had happened previously? Or just bits?'* She would soon find out. Nervously she glanced at her watch – the fifth time since finishing their meal. Now she her fears were taking a different route altogether. *It's' nearly time,'* she thought. *'Have they changed their mind?'*

"Am I too early? You did say half past." The voice

came from behind her, startling Clare. She turned towards it.

"No, no. We've only just finished. So glad you could come, Emily." They hugged. Clare invited Emily to sit next to her – between her and John. "Perfect timing," she said. "We just finished desert and are ready for coffees."

"There you are, Emily." It was John suddenly looking up from fiddling with his napkin and noticing what might have been a stranger. But it wasn't. He addressed her as if it were only yesterday that he had last seen her. Or perhaps more recently it would seem. "I was going to send someone into the bathroom after you," he added, his already wide smile breaking into a chuckle at his own joke.

Clare and Emily looked at each other as if to ask, *'What does he mean?'* Then they understood. He *hadn't* forgotten. Far from it, but what he *had* forgotten were the fifty years since he *had* last seen her. All those years were lost to him. To John, if they even existed at all they were as short as a simple trip to the bathroom.

Emily was too shocked to speak. *'He recognised me instantly,'* she pondered. *'But how?'* Even she could not deny that she had changed visually in the last fifty years.

Clare stepped in to cover for her. "Yes. It *is* Emily," she said, "but you haven't seen her for a long, long time."

"But she's my girl-friend," he said, with that puzzled look creeping back again. "Did she go somewhere?" Then, directly to Emily, "Tell me. Did you go somewhere? I thought you'd just gone to the bathroom. We've had desert. Coffee should be here soon." He was right about the last bit.

"Yes. I'm afraid I did go away, John my dear." Emily took hold of his hand as it rested on the table. Like her own, it was surprisingly smooth, hinting that life had been kind to them both.

"That's right," he said. "We broke up." It was all coming back to him now.

"We did. I'm so sorry."

"*You* broke up with *me*. Your Dad never did like me anyway." "Oh, he *did*," she insisted. "Mum too. They were just scared." "Scared? Of me?"

"Scared they'd lose me. That I'd leave them."

"So *I* lost *you*, and *you* left *me*? That was OK, I suppose. Yeh. I remember now. Broke my heart." John leaned forward to look briefly at her face, close in, searching for the answer she didn't have, then looked away. He loosened her hand from his so he could stare out of the window. Remembering.

After a moment of apparent reflection he turned back to her, leaning forward and with somewhat more intensity and passion, repeating. "Yes, you did. You broke my heart."

Clare looked on, powerless to help John deal with his emotions this time. '*Had she made a mistake?*' she asked herself for the tenth time. '*Is it too much for him?*' Her eyes lost focus as the first tears formed. John's tone and demeanour had shaken Clare perhaps more than it had Emily.

An almost tangible uncertainty swept over both women. Neither spoke, as both watched John reel from his own words. His gaze was now trained on the nodding tulips outside in the flower bed, seeming unable to cope with his inner turmoil.

"I am so sorry," Emily said, at last breaking the silence. "We were both so *young*."

John turned back to her now, composed. The grief that was so real fifty years ago had come back, but just for a moment. He was back with her again, now, as he reflected on lost years.

"They were good times," he said, now in a forgiving voice, taking hold of her hand in reassurance. "I loved you *so* much."

"I loved you, too, John. I hope you believe that. You must."

"Oh, yeh. 'Kids' love," he said. "The kind that never lasts."

That was how he had made it through the first time. It worked then, it should do now. But this time he wasn't *quite* so sure.

"I don't believe that – and neither should you," she whispered, conscious of where they were. "I've never stopped." Emily could hardly finish the words. She held John's hand again - even tighter. She really believed what she was saying, doubly so because she was confident to admit it to herself, to John, and even with Clare able to hear her.

Clare knew what she meant. She would have been worried – under normal circumstances. But these were *not* normal. "I think someone else has arrived," she said, relieved at the opportunity to break from the hold the two people had over her. "I'll just go and fetch them. You two stay here. You still have lots to talk about."

They did stay, John and Emily, lost in each other's thoughts. Finally John spoke. "It's my birthday, you know. They tell me I'm seventy five." He laughed at his own joke.

"You look so well, John," said Emily.

"I am. Physically. It's just this... (he struggled for the words)... this memory thing. I can't even remember what it's called. It's embarrassing."

"I'm sorry, John. For everything. Mum and Dad were sorry, too. They admitted it. Afterwards. I should have been driven by my own heart and feelings, and not their fears."

"Fifty years you say," said John. "Since we last met?" "That's right."

"Just as well," he said. "Otherwise you'd have been a long time in the bathroom."

They both laughed.

"You remembered then – this was the last time we were together. Here, in The Leather Bottle. We had dinner that time. Just the two of us."

"Amazing."

"It is," she agreed. "And it was. Unforgettable."

"No. It's amazing the restaurant has lasted as long as we have, what with fast-food taking over." He laughed at his own joke again. "I'm so glad it's still here to preserve old memories." He paused. "Remind me again. Fifty years ago. Why were we here?"

"It was your birthday," she added. "Fifty years to the day." "Still is. Every year. Same day – the first day of spring - or so

they tell me." Then his laughter stopped. His face

changed. "We broke up just a few days after. At least you didn't spoil my birthday."

"John? Someone else wants to meet you." It was Clare, returning from the lobby followed by a middle-aged man. "This is Joe," she said.

The tall, sandy-haired visitor reached forward. "Pleased to meet you, John," he said. "Happy birthday." They shook hands, then Joe took a seat at Clare's invitation.

"John?" said Emily, keen to get John's attention back. "This is my eldest son. Joe."

"Delighted to meet you," said John. "If you turn out anything like your mother, you'll be OK, apart from...." But his voice trailed off as if he had forgotten the rest of the sentence.

Or had he?

"John's at the university here," said Emily.

"He's a bit old for a student," John replied.

"Professor of English," broke in Joe. "I'm Head of the Literature Department."

"That's how we met, Clare and I," explained Emily, to John.

Clare was a part-time Admin. Assistant for the department and had been introduced to Emily, through Joe, at one of their 'Open Days'. As soon as Emily learnt of Clare's surname she asked the inevitable - did she know a John Sercombe?

It was there and then that the whole story came out. Emily was totally transparent with full details – or at least most of them – which Clare took on board as being 'something in the past'. She decided it would remain there. Over the weeks – leading up to

John's birthday – Clare and Emily became friends, close enough for them to agree on a plan - designed to help John tackle the dreaded Alzheimer's. John was to be reunited with Emily on his birthday - at The Leather Bottle where they had last met.

So far it had gone well. As time progressed more and more stories emerged, and were swapped. Clare took heart that John's memory seemed to be improving or, at least, was improved temporarily by the occasion. Clare had grown to know Joe as a close working colleague. They were soon wrapped in conversation, paying less attention to John and Emily, who reminisced at their precious times together leading up to their split exactly fifty years ago.

"Well, I'm afraid I have to love you and leave you," said Joe, finally. "I have a class in half an hour. Some of us still have to work."

"This really has been a good day, we *must* do this again," said Clare. Although she hated to admit it, the experience had provided a welcome relief for her and had clearly done John a power of good. She saw once again for the first time in years, the John she had met and had fallen in love with thirty years before.

"Can I make a suggestion?" asked Joe, getting up to leave.

"You're the Professor," said John. He, too, was enjoying this 'new kind of day' in his calendar.

"I have a significant birthday myself coming up in a few months time. Not until late October actually, but you must come to celebrate it with me."

"That sounds an excellent idea," agreed Emily. "We *all* must go!"

"Wouldn't miss it for the world," said Clare.

John seemed deep in thought, hesitating before he replied. "How significant is 'significant'?" he asked. Was he starting to put a few things together now? Events that had remained hidden for five decades? Would it lead to disclosures that were more than either Emily or Clare – or even Joe, for that matter – had anticipated?

"The big Five Zero," Joe replied.

"Fifty years ago?" John continued to turn the new information over and over in his head for a while longer until it dawned on him.

"Fifty years IS significant. It was certainly significant for us, wasn't it Emily?"

He caught Clare's eye, then looked at Emily before turning to Joe. "And I guess it's quite significant for us, Joe. It's turned into a really 'good day', as Clare would say.

"Hasn't it – son?"

~ *** THE END *** ~

Air and water - Averse

Air and water
We can't do without
It's sort of transparent
But we know it's about.
It's essential for living
And everyday life
I use it a lot
And so does my wife.

Keeping everything growing
On both land and sea
It's in every person...
Animal...and tree.
So we shouldn't pollute it
Or squander supplies
Lest the world that we live in
Disappears...and dies.

For it covers the earth
Over land...over sea
Bringing its riches
To both you and me.
I'm glad that we have it
I'm sure it will last
It secures a bright future
As it did in the past.

~ * * * ~

The Lifesaver
A short story with some truth in it

In 'The Black Rose of Blaby' I tell of one of the main characters saving the life of a toddler. As I have said previously I did pull someone out of the canal once. (Not counting the time Melv fell through the ice near the bridge close to the Premier Drum factory in Wigston, and I helped him up the bank.)

This time it must have been in the August holidays and I was putting in my ground bait prior to going fishing the next morning. I seem to recall my folks were on the 'annual fortnight holiday' which always took place on the same two weeks every year for each region in the country. Leicester's was the first two weeks in August before it was later brought forward to July.

I also remember walking and wheeling my bike along the towpath as I went about throwing in handfuls of groundbait prior to my returning to the same spots to fish in the coming days. It was then that this little girl – I guess she was about 8 years old – came running up shouting, "My brother's in the water!" Stirred into action by the urgency and panic in her voice, I followed her. We hastened to where her little brother had fallen into the canal.

We hadn't gone far before I saw this little bundle literally floating - pretty much on the surface of the water. Thank goodness, as I seem to recall, he was facing upwards – another blessing. And luckily, he was only a few feet from the bank, so I hardly got wet myself. (I could say I dived in, swam 100 yards in a torrent before adopting the life-saving hold to swim back carrying the unfortunate child. But that was not the case.)

He really *did* look just like a bundle of clothes – dressed in a woollen pullover that, so far at least, had not become saturated to the extent that there was a risk of dragging him beneath the surface. I quickly salvaged the poor wretch, checked that he had not swallowed any of the canal water, picked him up and placed him on my bike ready to walk the two little children to wherever they lived.

The children – the little girl and one other very small child – ran ahead, turning round every so often to make sure I was still following. We must have walked for about five minutes - along the tow path, across one of the locks, then a short distance into a housing estate. It was a council estate.

The boy I had pulled out of the canal seemed quite happy. I can see him now as he sat on my cross bar, staring into my face barely a foot away. He might have been getting a bit cold, though.

Arriving at their house, we continued up the front garden path and, I guess, someone must have rung the bell. What I *do* remember is the young mother coming to the door (not much older than I was) being besieged by all of us relating the story surrounding this "drama".

All the while, the mother was saying, "Oh, thank you mister," over and again.

"Mister"? I was still a teenager and not used to such accolade.

She then disappeared into a back room with a, "Hang on a minute, Mister", only to return clutching a ten shilling note. Amazing!

Now. Bearing in mind that this was the 1960's and even £10.00 was a decent weekly wage, this was quite an offering. My heart sank. Of course I could not – and did not – take it. I merely gave a polite "Thank You", closed the front door behind me, got on my bike and went back to laying my ground bait.

Clearly this made a big impression on me, even to this day. There was this young mother of three children who, I could tell, did not have much at all. Nevertheless, she was prepared to give me £25 in today's money for bringing her youngest home safely.

Footnote

I was working my way through college at the time. To do this I was a self-employed window-cleaner. My business covered a variety of types of houses, and customers. All too often I found the working class, and those with *the least to give* or pay, were the most honest and generous spirited. That, too, will never leave me.

* * *

The following is an account of a true event
involving a schoolmate in the 1960's

Dave Kettel – a true life-saver

Dave went to my school, Guthlaxton Grammar. Although he was not a high flyer academically, he always seemed decent, polite, and well brought up with good values.

How unfair was it therefore, when, being late for class in the afternoon – and not dressed in proper school uniform, - he was placed in detention? Dave being Dave, he apparently accepted it without complaint. Only at the detention session itself did the truth come out. It went like this:

Cycling back to school after lunch, along the canal tow path, he did notice someone in the water, in distress. In he dived fully clothed, saving the unfortunate non-swimmer. Secure in the knowledge that they were now safe, he cycled back home to change into dry clothes. Needless to say, he did not have a spare school uniform. Who did in those days? It was the 1960's after all.

All this came out on the afternoon of his detention. The next day – and let justice be done – his story was told to the whole school at morning assembly, by a very proud headmaster.

For those who remember Dave it would be for his blond – almost white – hair. You could say he was a trendsetter, wearing a signature hairstyle coveted by the soon-to-be 'cool' surfer boys. The resounding applause from the whole school led to his blushes being all the more noticeable, but that was Dave. Unassuming and modest to the last.

But the headmaster's joke was anything but cool. "If anyone else was thinking of such an heroic deed in the future, could they make sure they leave for school a half an hour earlier, in order not to be late for the bell."

It did *not* go down too well at all.

The first part is a true story.

*** ~ THE END ~ ***

The Coal-miner's Son

Life and times of a Kentucky mining family
in the 1930's

I live with my Ma and Pa plus two sisters and a brother. They're all younger than me – 'cept Ma and Pa, of course. 'spose you already guessed that. I'm fourteen years old and just about to leave school – such as it was. School, that is.

Apart from The Holy Bible and a Charles Dickens book (Pickwick Papers), the only other book we have in our house is the Sears and Roebuck catalog. I liked that as a kid because it had more pictures in it. I'm not sure which of the three books is furthest away from best describing *how* we live. That is to say, we're a God fearing family, but some of the stuff in any of them is either way out of reach of our comprehension, or unaffordable.

"Son," Ma would say, "if you want any more reading, you'd better write it yourself. But ask that city-born school teacher for the paper and pencil. We got no money for that, neither."

We live in Muhlenberg County – in Stom's Landing (named after the settler who first set up here), but which some folks have started calling *Paradise.* Maybe on account of the fact that they all have jobs there - courtesy of Peabody's Coal Train and the lumber yard – which depends on the Peabody mine.

I was the eldest at the time. I still am come to that, so it's because of me we've all become writers. Some say I tend to inspire people. Quite a feat for a poorly educated kid from a mining family in Paradise, Muhlenberg County. We all even had to learn how to spell correctly ourselves. There was no dictionary, so we used the three books I mentioned earlier – especially 'Sears' if it was a more modern word .

Spelling was a tad confusing sometimes anyway. Still is. When we first moved into the one-room shack near the mine where Pa worked, a mile out of town (and where we live now), the county was spelt 'Muhlenburgh' with a 'burgh' at the end - on account of the Scottish people who first settled there from Edinburgh.

Then a bunch of Germans came in, took over most of the jobs – and the houses ('*as well as the women folk*,' said Uncle Bill) – so it became MuhlenBERG. Originally we're from Virginia where the first English settled, so we could hardly understand either of them at first anyway – Scottish or German – so we kept to ourselves.

That's apart from Uncle Bill - my Pa's brother – who moved out here to be close to us and is almost part of the family. He's always raking around some place or other, though. That's where we get all the news, as interesting as *that* is, which is rarely. I love my Uncle Bill as much as I love Ma and Pa. Some days I love him even more, 'specially when he takes me fishin'. Pa never has time to do that anyway. And if he did have the time after working such long shifts, he'd be too tired.

"Make sure your Ma gets these fish," said Bill last time we were out. He gave me two of the ones he'd caught to add to my two. He lives on his own and doesn't need a lot. "They should keep you all fed for a couple of days."

He was right. I guess the catfish were only five or six pounds each, but they'd be tastier than the tough old twenty pounders some folks land. I wrote all this down in my notebook, like a diary. Come winter and we would be kept indoors most days on account of the weather, I would read about what we did in the summer. The schoolteacher has always encouraged me to do that at school – 'to inspire others' she would say.

Usually she's mighty strict with all us kids – having to cope with young 'uns only six years old right up to fourteen year olds like me – often bigger than her, even some of the girls. She came from the big city to teach 'where she's needed most' she revealed one time. I think the way we live and the fact that we can hardly keep a decent pair of boots on our feet right through winter shocked her a bit at first. She soon toughened up, though and, despite her being strict most of the time, she always softened up whenever I read to the class. And to her. I tried to please her with what I wrote, mindful that she had little to to cheer her otherwise.

Often I'd read my diary out loud to my brother and sisters – and to Ma if she was in the kitchen, baking. Pa would be down in the mine and be too tired to even listen in the evenings after supper. I tried a few times but he always fell asleep beside the stove. Becky said maybe it was *because* I read to him he dozed off. I don't *think* she meant it – not in a bad way.

Becky's a year younger than me. I love her too –

like a sister. Then there's *her* younger sister, Annie, followed by Jason, who's nine years old. To hear Ma and Pa talk, there won't be any more 'McAllisters'. That's my name by the way, *Jamie* McAllister.

Like I said we all write. That's how we amuse ourselves, and amuse other people. I hope so, anyway. Becky and Annie sometimes read out loud what they've written, but it's mostly girls stuff, which you'd expect, I guess. Ma listens to them especially hard, though. I suppose because she was a girl once. Her name's Doreen, *I think*. I say 'I think' because it's only Billy who calls her by that name. Occasionally.

Pa calls her 'Ma', same as us. Neighbours call her Mrs McAllister, at least in front of us kids. As for Pa's name, I simply have no idea what that is. Billy calls him 'Bro'. Ma calls him Pa, same as us. Neighbours call him – *you guessed it* – Mister McAllister. That's apart from his boss, or the sheriff, who shorten it to '*McAllister*'.

Pa says the sheriff is always snooping around and we should tell him if we see his car parked up in the nearby woods. Pa says it's on account of Billy and what he gets up to. Apart from Ma and Pa, I'm the only one in the family who knows *what* Billy gets up to. But they don't know I know, even though Billy does, but he doesn't know that Ma and Pa don't know that I know. But I'll tell you. *(If you want me to explain that again, I will. Or you can go back and re-read it - slowly.)*

It's moon-shining. Billy's got a still out in the back shed – *our* back shed next to where we keep the dogs. Billy's dogs. They don't get out much mainly because they keep guard. *It also keeps them sharp*, Pa reckons. When we go fishing I always ask Billy if we can take them with us. He says, *OK, as long as Jason keeps look-out for the sheriff*. It never occurred to them that, one day, Jason might actually want to know *why* he needs to keep look-out. So far, he hasn't asked.

I said Billy lives on his own. That's only partly true. He's not *married* or anything, but sometimes I can see he's had somebody round. By somebody I mean a woman – female - unless whatever guy he has round leaves a bright red lipstick mark on the liquor glass they've been drinking out of! I very much doubt *that,* and I'm pretty sure I know who *she* is. It's the daughter of the guy who runs the bar in town where Billy delivers his moonshine. She's the only one I've seen who paints herself up. (Ma says it's disgusting and that she's only as good as she ought to be – whatever *that* means.)

In fact I *know* I'm right about who she is. The drinking glass with a red stained rim is always left next to the sink the days *after* Billy delivers his moonshine to the bar in town.

"She don't mean nothin' to me," he told me one day, even though I didn't ask. He just saw the way I looked at the dirty glass. Billy knows how my mind works – even more than Ma, or Pa. More than me, even.

I know he *did* have someone special, back-along, who *did* mean something. Ma told me. I asked her, "How come Billy lives on his own?" That's when she told me the whole story.

She was the sister of the guy who ran the sawmills,

Ma started. *At least he* said *she was his sister. She was a real looker, but never had a beau – not* one *that anybody knew about, anyway. It was her brother who kept them away.* 'Nobody is good enough for her,' *he used to say. He was high-born. So was she. Weekends and holidays he would go back to Greenville on his own, where the family had a big house. That's where he had a wife, or so they say.*

Then Ma went on to say how, at weekends, the sister – Eleanor her name was – would *never* go into Greenville with him. Soon the trouble started. Without her brother to keep an eye on her she would sneak off to the bar in Paradise, letting her hair down as it were. But word got out to her brother. Ralph was *his* name, the brother.

Billy was a lot younger then, said Ma, *and wild. He could drink, too, and not just moon-shine. The bar was his favourite place and, of course, he was single. Pa stopped going out drinking with him on account of the fights Billy started. But Billy saved and bought the land and cabin where he is now, and had taken over the 'Shine' business once old man Newton – the one who had it before - decided to give it all up. New responsibility calmed him down some.*

Of course, it was all illegal, so he kept a few pigs and goats as a front, hiding what he was really up to. Like a smokescreen. To add to that he took a job at the sawmills. As you can imagine, it was all working out well for Billy. He had Eleanor to himself at weekends when Ralph was in Greenville; then during the week he could sneak around at the sawmill as long as her so-called brother didn't find out. But it didn't last.

That was as much as Ma told me, or wanted me to know. It was Billy himself who opened up to me one day we were out fishing. It was after a weird thing happened that really spooked him. Me too. We had just finished fishing and were about to pack up when he froze.

"Did you see that?" he asked, suddenly becoming agitated. He pointed out across the lake where the sunset had sent a golden path, ending at the exact spot where were were standing. Then he spoke again – but not to me this time - and started to walk into the water.

"I'm coming," he said, dropping his fishing rod. I thought, '*Who's he talking to?*'

I knew it wasn't me, but I couldn't see anyone else. It was just us two as far as I could tell. By now he had waded out until he was waist deep, about twenty feet from the bank. "I'm coming, darlin'," he repeated, but the 'darlin' bit told me he must be seeing *someone*, and that 'someone' was female.

"Uncle Billy, stop!" It was me shouting now and, thank God he was listening because he did. He stopped where he was, waist high. He looked down and had this puzzled look on his face, as if he didn't understand how he got there. Or why. Which was right, of course.

He turned, "Jamie? That you?" He was looking at me now, still looking confused, as if he had just discovered I was also there. The sun had now dipped below some clouds on the horizon. The path of sunlight had dissolved. It had gotten darker. "Did you see her too?" He asked.

"See who, Billy?"

"Eleanor. She was there. Walking towards me."

"On the water? Are we talking about an Eleanor, or whatever her name is? Or Jesus?" Ma would have given me a slap if she'd heard me refer to Him in such a disrespective way, but all Billy was interested in was whoever it was he'd seen.

"You should have let me go on," said Billy. "She's gone now, thanks to you. Why did you stop me? " He looked down, woefully sad as he made his way back to the bank, and just sat. He kept his eyes pointed down on the floor and as soon as I saw his shoulders shaking, I knew it was serious. Whatever 'it' was.

I sat next to him, searching his face but all I could see at first was somebody I didn't know. For the first time in his life he looked lost. "There was nobody there," I said.

"She comes for me - sometimes." He wasn't looking down any more, nor out to the lake, nor at me. He was just vacant. Staring straight ahead at – nothing.

"But I thought they said she was -"

"- dead?" he said. "No. She just has to keep away, in case they come looking for her."

"Who are 'they' and why are they looking for her?"

"They think she did it. Killed him."

"Ralph?" I'd heard he'd been found dead, at the sawmills.

"They'd been arguing. Later he was found face down in the mud outside one of the timber sheds. It had broken his neck – the fall that is. He must have fallen from the loft."

"An accident, then?" I said.

"Could have been. Then his wife showed up and tried to make out he'd been killed. Murdered she reckoned. Apparently she'd found out about Eleanor. Turns out she – Eleanor - wasn't his sister after all."

"Why didn't they arrest her?"

"Eleanor?"

"Yeah." I could see Billy was more agitated just thinking about it.

"They reckon she didn't wait around long enough. Just left before the sheriff could get a warrant." Billy stood up then, burying his face in his hands. "I didn't mean to do it." He was sobbing again, this time uncontrollably.

I had never seen Billy like this before. I did nothing. I just stood there feeling stupid. Several minutes later he straightened up, collecting his fishing gear and catch. So did I. We began to walk.

"Sorry," he said as we headed back to his place.

We continued the rest of the way in silence. Apart from the loons on the lake and the occasional buzzard cry overhead, the only other sound was the swishing of our boots brushing the undergrowth. We carried on through the woods until we could smell the woodsmoke from the pot belly stove in his cabin. We knew we were close. The cabin finally came into view. His two hounds rushed ahead, hoping for some reward. Food, probably.

The catfish weighed heavy in my sack as I said goodbye to Billy intent on making my way back home, whistling for the hounds to follow. But not before he could finish his story. Guilt was weighing heavier on his shoulders as the catfish were on mine. He needed to offload. So I helped.

"He just came at me," said Billy, continuing where he had left off some half an hour earlier. "He'd seen me and Eleanor that day, during my break, We weren't doing anything we shouldn't have, but he could tell we had something. He knew we had *something*. Eleanor and me were up in the loft in one of the timber stores, just talking. But close. He'd have none of it. We argued and all kinds of stuff came out. *Bad* stuff. In a jealous rage he just ran at me waving one of the log splitters.

"All I did was just step aside, but he carried on – right through the loft opening. We must have been over fifteen foot up, high enough so that stuff could be easily loaded onto carts below.

"Landing on his head didn't help. He wouldn't have felt a thing."

"But Uncle Billy, what *could* you have done? It was either you or him!"

"Stayed, is what I should have done," he said, "instead of running. People heard his scream as he fell. They ran over to the barn where we were. They soon gathered round - before we could think. She said for me to run out back and that she'd take care of it. But they turned on her. Accusing her."

"Then what happened?"

"Someone said to call the sheriff. That's when - or so they told me afterwards - she turned and ran too. Before he could come with a warrant." Billy was now shaking, barely able to make the words as he recalled those last tragic moments.

"Ma said she died after jumping into the Green River and drowning, trying to get away from the bloodhounds."

"That's what I heard, too," he said, " but nobody saw her jump. Or fall. The hounds just took the sheriff's men to the water's edge – where the scent ended – and couldn't pick it up from there. Her body was never found."

~ *** ~

That was seven years ago.

I am now going on twenty one years old – nearly a man (!) - and working in The Greenville Leader as a trainee reporter. That's on account of me turning up one day and seeing the editor guy with my portfolio of writing. He liked what I was writing but, most of all, he liked the way I got through to see him. He said I had perseverance and hired me on the spot. I've been here nearly twelve months.

Pa was disappointed that I didn't go down the mine to feed Peabody's Coal Train (!) alongside him, but Ma was pleased. She saw what Black Lung had done to Pa. Barely forty and he looked sixty – worn out. And that cough of his didn't sound too special. Only Billy's moonshine seemed to help.

I suppose that's why I always turned to his brother, Billy, because he loved the outdoors even more than I did. *There's no way I'm going down that hole*, he said, meaning the mine. A lot of the time, though, they stripped the *surface* of the land for their coal, taking out trees and anything else that got in their way. That's how Billy always managed to find work in the timber yards.

Because I had a job now it cut down my fishing trips with Billy, but we still got away some evenings, and at weekends during the winter. But I still recall how he told me about Eleanor after his vision on the lake that one time.

He told me it wasn't the first time he'd seen her after that day Ralph was killed and she had disappeared. But she always vanished soon after she appeared. She seemed more ghost than real person and, because some said she *was* dead, he took her to be her spirit reaching out to him – but from where?

My first job at The Leader, apart from opening the post and acting as a 'Gopher' in the office, was copy-editing – reading the whole edition before it went to print, picking out spelling mistakes and other errors. I had become quite good at it so I carried on doing it. Not only did that mean I knew all that was going on in the world, but I knew all that was for sale and who was who - all through the advertisements.

Doing what I do every day – reading the newspaper – means that I get to notice recurring stories. A favourite one, it seems, is the appearance of Bigfoot, Goatman, or some other mythical or mystical being. These sightings, true or false, always seem to be made out in the woods, or on deserted country lanes and come in clusters. One report is usually followed by several soon after. Usually they are of some monster or giant or animal-like shape-shifter. The one I am about to tell you about was different.

It was a woman.

Now that rarely happens. The other thing that caught my interest was that, although the locations of the sightings varied, they remained in roughly the same area. None of them were actually *in* Paradise, but they were in the general area *outside* of the town, and usually not far from the Green River.

Sometimes there were noises and disturbances at night around remote cabins or settlements. Or backpackers camping overnight. The next morning people would wake up to discover clothing left outside gone, or the hen house raided with eggs taken or – on occasions – even the hens themselves. But never money or valuable possessions.

When it got particular bad, and if there were a lot of reports, locals would get together and go on a search. They always came back empty handed, not having seen any stranger, or being, or animal. The only exception was when they would come across an abandoned cabin or a shelter used by trappers, or hunters for an over-night camp – where there was evidence of someone living there. There were a few of these scattered around the woods, often places where wood-cutters had lived, or charcoal-burners who provided fuel for iron smelting, before coal took over and they left.

I told Billy about this because I had a funny feeling about it. *What if?* I thought. *What if Eleanor had not died after all, but had survived and stayed close to the places she knew?* He agreed it was possible so we decided to do some exploring of our own that weekend. We'd take off Friday night and stay overnight – camping out – until Sunday. We took heart that it could be her when some of the sightings talked about a woman with long red hair, but they had seen little else to identify her.

Eleanor had red hair. *I'd look across at her sometimes when we were out and,* Billy said, *if the sun was behind her, the light shining through her hair made it look as though it was on fire.* There were a few redheads in the area, mainly due to the Scottish coming over and settling in Airdrie Hill, but over the decades red or auburn hair became rare due to inter-marriages.

Billy and me set out early that Friday evening. It was June, so there was plenty of light left and it was warm. We didn't bother packing much more than a bedroll each, intending to camp out under the stars or under the trees, seeing as how there little chance of rain. We weren't short of wood, either, so we could keep a fire burning for most of the night. If that wasn't enough to keep us warm, Billy had brought along supplies of moonshine.

Our first instinct was to head for the river. You always need water. By the second day we had covered probably twenty miles without any sign of the unusual, male or female. That evening we did happen upon one of those cabins I was talking about. It was derelict but still in reasonable shape, leastways the roof was. Best of all it had a stove. "Shall we make this our next camp?" I asked. "It'll be dark in an hour anyway." Billy agreed.

We lit the stove, took out the night's provisions, then sat. Talking. I had taken along a few newspaper clippings to show Billy. All he had to go on were the stories I'd told. We figured we would keep a lamp burning – even through the night. That was because if there *was* someone in the woods, curiosity would get the better of them and they would check out who these strange visitors – us – were.

Again we talked some, but soon the effect of Billy's moonshine together with our tiredness got the better of us. I have no idea whether it was Billy or me who dropped off to sleep first. All I was aware of was Billy shaking me gently, and at the same time whispering for me to keep my voice down and my movements soft.

There was someone outside.

An occasional hoot of an owl or the scream of its prey if it had caught some unfortunate victim was all the sound there was. The rest of the time – most of the time – it was dead quiet. Even the breeze had dropped so the leaves hardly stirred.

But something did. You could just *sens*e it.

Was it a bear? Black bears were common and favourites for scavenging waste bins. Unlike grizzlies, they rarely attacked unless startled. They had excellent noses for left-over scraps.

But we had left no food outside.

Coyotes were also a nuisance, often a noisy nuisance, but only food would attract them. There were no wolves, and cougars tended to keep away from humans. The odds were that the intruder – if they were intent on intruding – was human.

Hopefully only one of them.

There were two windows either side the door and a bright moon that night. It peaked shyly through the canopy of leaves above. Billy took one window, me the other, peering carefully from the edge of each window so we couldn't be seen from the outside. There was a clearing just a few yards in front of the cabin. It was lit by the moon. "Shhh," said Billy. "What's that over there?" he pointed to the edge of the clearing. I could see a bush moving, but only slightly as if they were conscious of being watched.

The dog that skipped out from the undergrowth had heard us and ran towards the cabin. Its sharp bark outvoted by its wagging tail. A small figure followed soon after, "Jake, come here!" whispered a voice. It was a girl, a young girl, perhaps six years old. The dog ignored her so she ran after it, slipping a piece of rope through its collar.

"Stay here!" hissed Billy not before I could open the door to the cabin. I was gone and he was too late. As soon as the girl saw me she stopped in her tracks, thinking about her next move.

"Don't be scared," I said to the young girl, but softly, anticipating that she was wondering whether to run or, her curiosity getting the better of her, stay to find out 'who was this stranger in her woods'?

I stepped off the porch onto the grassy covering of the clearing. She stopped, turning to face me. I knelt down, now the same height as she was. Her dog continued to wag his tail. She was being brave but she *looked* scared. "I won't hurt you." I reached out to her with my open hand.

"If you *do* hurt her, if you so much as *touch* her, it'll be the last thing you do, pretty boy," said a voice still hidden in the darkness, beyond the clearing. It was the voice of a woman – and one with good taste at that, but all I could see was a rifle barrel.

And it was pointing right at me.

I wasn't in the mood to argue, so I froze. She crept slowly forward out of the shade and into the moonlight, as the little girl ran up to her. "Mamma," she cried, "I only wanted to look."

"That's OK," said the woman as the little girl hid behind her long coat. "Just stay close. OK baby girl?"

The girl nodded.

" I just wanted to..." I began.

"All I hear is *want*! Nobody's interested in what *you* want, pretty boy. I just need to know why you're here." She was armed, but the way she spoke belayed her own fear matching mine.

I was still crouched, even lower now. She came forward towards me, still a safe distance away but she stood looking down at me. That's when I saw what Billy had described earlier. The moon was above us both now, the woman and me, its light shining through her hair from behind – through her *red* hair – creating a halo.

"Eleanor?"

Billy took *that* word right out of my mouth. He was still at the cabin, watching the scene as it unfolded, but now from outside on the front porch. He had a clearer view of the woman than I did.

The woman, or at least her hair, was still bathed in an aura of light, from a pale yellow on the edges to a rich auburn as it framed her face. She was indeed the beauty she had been made out to be. But still I didn't move, the rifle remained trained on me.

"Is that you, Billy?" she asked, the hard tone of

her voice now softening as she recognised first the voice – then the figure - on the porch. Much to my relief she lowered the rifle, but still held the little girl close.

"I thought you were dead," he replied. "They told me..." His voice trailed off. Still he stayed on the porch, unmoving. He was stunned, still not believing the vision standing before him.

She hesitated. "I was," she said. " I am, to the world anyway." She peered into the shadow cast by the overhang to the porch where Billy stood, searching for more of his familiar features. " How have you been, Billy?"

"Lousy," he said. There was no emotion in his voice, apart from maybe despair.

Finally he made his way – slowly – to where she and the little girl stood. Enshrouded in the discovery of each other they remained oblivious to everything and everyone around them. He reached out to take her free hand. She dropped the rifle so he could take the other.

Meanwhile I was getting cramp.

"Can I move now?" I asked.

"Just as you like, pretty boy." But it was Billy who spoke, picking up on Eleanor's new name for me. It was she who made the next move, taking his grizzled face in her hands before drawing him close. "Hold me," was all she said.

Billy didn't need asking twice. The seven years that had passed, without her and without his knowing she was alive, had been the longest years of his life. They held each other as the years they had been apart gradually melted away, until it was the little girl who spoke.

"Who's this man, Mamma?"

"This is your... Billy," she said, loosening her hold to wipe away a tear before the little girl noticed.

"*My* Billy?" she questioned. "he looks a lot like *your* Billy," said the little girl. "You mean we got to *share* Billy?"

"She's got your wacky sense of humour," said Eleanor without any explanation. Billy was coming up with answers in his head to his own imagined questions, ones he hadn't even asked yet. And he would find many to ask.

"Shall we go inside?" I suggested, seeing my chance. "It's getting a tad chilly out here." We made our way into the cabin; me, Billy and Eleanor arm in arm, followed by the little girl, and Jake.

"Is that the smell of coffee? *Real* coffee?" asked Eleanor as the warmth of the cabin greeted us. "It's been all too long." We were later to learn what she had meant, living as she had as a virtual hermit.

"You don't look any different," said Billy.

"Apart from the Daniel Boone outfit, you mean?"

She was dressed in buckskin, coat and pants, with leather boots and a narrow brimmed hat. A Bowie knife was slung from her belt.

"I wasn't going to mention that part, but..." said Billy.

Eleanor went on to fill us in on the last seven years of her life. Apparently she had nearly drowned trying to cross the Green River to escape the hounds. She hadn't swum far before tiredness dragged her downstream where she landed on the shore on the very same side from which she had started. Luckily, by then the bloodhounds had lost her scent.

It was there, unconscious through exhaustion, that an old Cherokee woman had found her and taken her in. She was a throwback from when the Indian Nation populated Kentucky, but she had avoided being relocated in a reservation. She was a young girl then. Now she was ancient, having survived ever since by relying on her backwoodsman skills and Cherokee upbringing. She lived on her own deep in the woods. Nobody ever bothered her, and she never bothered anybody else.

But that day she *did* bother. She helped Eleanor back to her shelter – a reclaimed charcoal-burner's cabin. It was there that she helped Eleanor with the birth of her little girl, Awanita. It meant 'fawn' in Cherokee but they had shortened it to 'Nita'. The Cherokee woman delivered the baby after showing Eleanor the 'Indian ways' of childbirth. What she had not already learnt from the women of her tribe before she was parted from them, she developed her own skills in natural medicines, herbs and, through necessity, surviving on what she could catch, forage, or grow. She passed these on to Eleanor.

Eleanor knew there would still be a warrant out for her so she also decided to stay away from normal civilisation for as long as it took. She explained everything to the Cherokee woman, who had no love for the American (or English, German or Scottish, as it were) people.

She learned how to survive from her host, and the three lived together for a further five years until the Cherokee woman died, quietly, of old age. She and Nita were now on their own.

"Nita and me have been on our own now for over a year," said Eleanor. "We get by the best we can, but Nita needs schooling, other peoples. She needs kids her own age."

"You can come back with us," said Billy.

"T'wouldn't be fair on you," she replied. "If I get caught you'd go to jail. But you could take Nita. Bring her up as your own."

"I'm not leaving without you," said Billy.

They both fell silent. I said nothing. Nita – and Jake – were both fast asleep in front of the stove. Soon it would be light and the dawn chorus was beginning. Eventually Eleanor spoke.

"I meant it when I said you could bring her up as your own. She *is* 'your own' anyway. She's your daughter. Have you forgotten what the argument was about when..." She didn't finish the sentence. She meant when Ralph took a swallow dive out of the loft.

"... how could I forget?" Billy said.

"They would both be safe at your place, Billy," I said. "Nobody ever goes out to see *you*."

"'cept you," smiled Billy.

I was crossing the line now, but I didn't care. "It's not just about you two any more," I said. "You have to think about Nita. She deserves a future. A normal upbringing."

Billy and Eleanor looked at each other. I knew I was right. So did they. "The boy's got a point," Billy said.

"Not just a pretty face," she replied. Nobody said another word. We made what was left of the breakfast provisions make do for four, but Eleanor drained the last of the coffee pot.

"Are you any good with a still?" Billy asked, turning to Eleanor.

"Where d'you think I got this red hair from?" she answered. We struck out for Paradise, and home.

And that's how Billy got himself a wife and family...

~ * * * THE (HAPPY) END * * * ~

Grandad - A song by John Morey

(If sung – use the tune of 'Pancho and Lefty' by Townes Van Zandt – not given here for reasons of copyright)

This is actually about my GREAT Grandad. He, and then his son owned the tailor's shop in Exmouth at 10, The Parade from the end of the 1800's.

The story goes, according to my Dad, that when Buffalo Bill's Wild West Show was in town – more likely in or near Exeter – Big Chief Sitting Bull and some of his braves visited Morey's the Tailors.

If it is true – IF – then it supports the theory that most of us (in this case, me!) are only 3-4 steps away from someone famous. In my case that would mean General Custer who met his fate at the Battle of Little Big Horn all those years ago.

C
Grandad came to Exmouth town
   G
To find a place and settle down
F
Brought his wife and family
  C   G
A brand new start beside the sea
F
A Master Tailor was his trade
C   F
They all loved the suits he made
Am   F   G
With velvet cuffs and silk brocade
    F   Am

The fashions of the day

All he wanted was a pleasant life
A fine young boy, a charming wife
He worked hard, his business thrived
The envy of any man alive
Then one day he felt a thrill
(Of) the Wild West Show of Buffalo Bill
So excited he couldn't wait, until
The show arrived in town

F
He was a dreamer of that it's true
C   F
He loved his wife and his family too
Am   F   G
Regrets he had were but a few
        F   Am
He was lucky I suppose

The show arrived he bought their seats
Front row, champagne, all the treats
He didn't worry about the cost
Or the opportunity would be lost
When he thought his cup was full
They introduced him to Chief Sitting Bull
With his braves he came next day
To buy a suit of clothes

He was a dreamer of that it's true
He loved his wife and his family too
Regrets he had were but a few
He was lucky I suppose

His fame had spread beyond belief
The tailor to a nation's Chief
The local man fulfilled his dream
With every stitch and every seam
But scarlet fever made him sick
His death as cruel as it was quick
As life delivers you one last kick
Your memories fade away

He was a dreamer of that it's true
He loved his wife and his family too
Regrets he had were but a few
He was lucky I suppose

The story I've just told is true
It could have happened to me or you
We have to take our chance and dare
In the time we are here or there
I never met my old Grandad
But I often wish I had
His life was short and that makes me sad
But he was lucky I suppose...

~ * * * ~

Paul

A poem of friendships, and the debt I still owe

I woke up slowly from a gentle sleep
And thought of Paul,
Who I had known some forty years before
For just a short time.
We were friends then - and would be now
If time and separation had not interfered.

Or did ambition take us somewhere else?

I remembered the pain he had suffered which I
could not heal.
Did I try?
Obviously not enough - with me left with this guilt.
It must have been real to survive so many years.
But the cause?
For him, Love for a woman.
(It very often was. For many of us.)
In his case it was Wendy who he loved *so much*.
His hurt was shared equally. And by us all.

It wasn't that *she* didn't love *him*.
She probably did, but he simply didn't know it.
Not for certain.
Meanwhile, we, their friends, were all fine.
He saw what we had. And just hoped.
The love tore him – them - apart.
We simply watched. We looked without seeing.
I remember his pain and hers, now of course,
As I awake from my gentle sleep with new insight.

They, whoever "they" are, talk about the heart
When referring to the ache I now carry.
It should be their pain, Paul and Wendy's - and still
may be.
Now it is mine too.
As it should have been back then.
If I had listened.

Before I allowed this pain, this ache, to wash over
me again, I had been thinking of Paul and the good
times we shared back then.
We laughed so much, so hard, but over what?

Apart from fleeting visions
I strain to flash up full versions of the past.
That past.
Memories may have faded but the joy remains
Of those happy hours.
Events I cannot even prove happened.

I guess *that* is what makes events so special.
(As the rare, the uncertain, the unproven, simple
beliefs, often are.)
Some call it faith.

To call it a connection, of friendship, is not enough.
To call it a debt is also wrong, but I do owe
Something.
But I am unsure as 'to whom'.

It's part of what I am now. What I have become.
Yes, I owe something, to those I have touched

And to those who have touched me.
Albeit briefly.

Paul, Wendy – how many more are out there – good people
Lurking to face me after a gentle sleep?
To ponder that now would only dilute
What I have now, and need to address.

Just laying down these thoughts, Dear Reader,
Is helping me soften the pain, the ache.
But, I hope, it will not dispel the joy of rediscovering a friendship I had forgotten
And one that may still be out there.

But where?
And what if Paul and I were to meet after so long?

Would I say, "Is the pain still there? Can I help?"

And he, in turn, might reply
"No matter. It has done its work.
(Referring to 'time'.)
And, because of it, we are what we have become."

~ * * * ~

Peregrine the Peregrine

Foreword

The following tale is a departure from the author's normal genre – romantic novel writing.

Inspired by actual happenings on one of his many country walks, the tale is a work of fiction, albeit rooted to a degree in reality. The following events did happen, apart from the shouting (talking) – as far as any human can safely say.

It should also be understood that the author does not set himself up as an expert ornithologist. With that in mind, any departures from the exact nature and behaviour of the main characters – birds – will, hopefully be forgiven.

Younger readers in particular should consult friends and family who do have knowledge of bird behaviour. If that fails, the RSPB welcomes aspiring birdwatchers and naturalists – or they can always visit the Bowling Green Marsh near Topsham, Exeter.

Peregrine the Peregrine – a moral tale

Peregrine was tucking into his prey. It was a shoveler duck. There were quite a few of them by the waterside that day – on the nature reserve near Topsham, on Bowling Green Marsh.

His stoop had been impressive – descending at close on 200 mph as he could – not *just* to show off to the other birds what he could do when he put his mind to it – but to snatch the unfortunate bird on the lake without any hitch in the operation. (He hated it when – but only on rare occasions – he 'missed' his prey, much to the delight of Jim Crow and his family. This time he was proud of his dive. What's more, he always liked to put on another show exclusively for the birdwatchers in the hide just across the water – especially as it was a Saturday. It was usually a 'full house' at weekends.

Of course, the 'guardians of the marsh', the redshank, never help – coming out with their 'skee, skee' alarm call if they happened to catch sight of him out hunting. 'Taking a recky,' you might say. '*This time you were just a little bit too late,*' he mused to himself but aimed at the redshank who were just a little bit late with their warning on this occasion. Settling himself by the waterside, he set about devoiding the bird of its plumage. He was well away by the time an interruption to his repast arrived.

"'allo," came a voice, startling him for a second, he was *so* engrossed in his meal. He always got carried away at the plucking stage. For him it was almost like a meditation – a Zen experience. As he once said to his mate, when asked what he liked best about it, he said, "'I find my 'happy place'."

"Caw! What have you got there?" It was that voice again. The peregrine recognised it at once, which is why he was trying to ignore it. But in vain. The owner of the voice would *not* go away, so eventually he gave in.

"'allo yerself, Jim Crow," he replied.

"Nice looking bird," said Jim.

"Thanks. You're not so bad yourself." The

peregrine had to force himself to answer, so he thought he might as well be pleasant. It was his idea of a joke but, obviously, crows were not as bright as falcons. Or were they? But the crow didn't even raise a smile, let alone laugh – I guess he was loathe to give the peregrine the satisfaction.

Finally, the peregrine's curiosity got the better of him. "What d'ya want, Jimbo?"

"A bit of civility would be nice," answered the crow. "How do you know who I am, anyway?"

"*Everybody* knows who *you* are," replied Peregrine. "Are you still with the same bird?"

"Jan, you mean?"

"That's the one." The peregrine ceased de-feathering the shoveller for a moment, turning to make sure it was who he thought it was. "Not that I'd recognise her."

"Why's that?" asked Jim.

"You all look the same to me – and you don't age so well."

"Charming! I could say that about you. You've all got the same markings," the crow replied, a little testily this time. "And there's no need to be racist!"

The peregrine paused for a while, exasperated. He was only half way through preparing his feast and had yet to get to the meat. All he had so far were feathers. "Yes?" he asked, locking the crow in his stare, pressing for a reason why he had been disturbed from his very important task. In any case he was hungry, not having eaten for hours.

Jim Crow was getting to the point, eventually. "What's your name, anyway?" he asked. "You never *did* say."

"Peregrine."

"No!" Jim was getting flustered again. "What's your *name. Who* are you, not *what* are you. I know you're a peregrine."

"I just said – Peregrine."

"Peregrine the peregrine?"

"That's what I said." He continued plucking.

"Well, I'm glad that's settled," said the crow.

There was a long pause while Peregrine continued to prepare his meal, leaving Jim Crow time to think of something else to say. Or do. He decided to 'do' – creeping forward to get a whiff, or even a sight, of the deceased shoveller.

"Careful, Sunshine," hissed Peregrine, without looking up or interrupting his rhythm. "You don't want to be next on my dinner table, do you?"

Jim Crow stopped in his tracks. He stepped back, ready to make his escape, just in case... Peregrine had reached the meaty bits. It made him even more wary and aggressive. After a while Jim Crow mustered enough courage to pose his next question. He began tentatively, almost whispering.

"I don't suppose -" he paused, "you could spare -"

"No!" snapped the falcon. "Get your own!" With that he lunged at the crow. He hadn't noticed Jan Crow creeping up on the other side, ready to snatch a morsel or two of prime shoveller – but he turned back to what he had been doing, just in time to catch her out. "Off!" he screamed, feigning a 'yarak'.

The falcon had extended his talons, in typical 'yarak' fashion, capable of ripping off the tail feathers of the crow – or worse – but he just wanted to scare her this time.

"Caw! You're in a mood, ain't ya?" Jan said, moving back to a safer distance.

'Women!' Muttered Jim, witnessing the failure.

"Some of us work for a living," was the falcon's reply to Jan.

"How about swapsies?" asked Jim.

"Depends. Wadda ya got?"

"That's a very nice Al Pacino impression, Perry old boy," said Jim, rather cheekily this time, with just a tad of David Niven about him. Then he replied with, "I do a nice line in sheep's eyeballs..."

"*No* thank you." Peregrine was quite adamant. The last thing he, or any bird of prey for that matter, wanted, was the local farmer accusing him of raiding his sheep and cattle. Crows were notorious for this particular nasty practice, especially at lambing time. Hooking their talons into the top of the sheep's head before... The falcon shuddered at the thought and carried on with his meal.

"How's the missus?" asked Jim, trying to open up another line of conversation.

"Not seen her," answered Peregrine, his mouth full of shoveller.

"Caw! You don't half 'shovel it in'," said Jim Crow in the way of a joke. Then, "Geddit?" he added, chuckling.

"So where *is* the missus?" Jim persisted.

"Dunno," replied Peregrine. "It's not mating season yet. Why should I care? She always turns up when it's time."

"I thought you were like us and mated for life.

The same wife."

"We do. But I like my own space as well." Peregrine was starting to 'open up' – Jim Crow was trying to get his trust.

"I get that, I *really* do," said the crow. "I'm a bit like that myself. I do go off on my own, sometimes, but me and Jan would miss each other if we weren't together *most* of the time."

Fool!, said Peregrine, to himself.

It was Jan who came right out with it, "Are you going to eat *all* that?" she asked, pointing at the remains of Peregrine's lunch.

"Listen, Mrs.," he said, walking towards the female crow, threateningly. In so doing, he inadvertently – without realising – left his lunch unguarded. Jim was in like a flash, grabbing a wing which, unfortunately, was still attached to the rest of the shoveller. It was heavier than he imagined. As soon as he tried to launch – or should we say 'lunch'! - into flight, the weight of the waterfowl dragged him down again. He dropped it.

"Curses!" yelled Jim. With that, Peregrine was onto both of them, chasing both Jim and Jan across the meadow. It was their downfall. All of them.

But they were being watched...

"Bingo!" It was Barrie the Buzzard. He had been watching the game from afar – on the tall hedgerow at the far end of the meadow. He made his move, swooping low and silently no more than six feet above ground, camouflaged and undetected by the hedge in the background.

"Hey, you!" cried Peregrine, catching the sight of Barrie out of the corner of his eye after he finally chased off Jim and Jan.

"Yeh, you!" joined in Jim and Jan together, even more upset at seeing their hoped-for chances of a free meal disappear, "that's ours."

"Was," replied Barrie through his beak. "It's mine, now." Being a much bigger bird, Barrie was a lot stronger than either the crows or, indeed, the falcon. Peregrine gave chase but it was only a token challenge – a mere gesture. He had eaten enough wildfowl for one day anyway so he let the buzzard run off with his prize.

"There was only gristle left," he muttered sulkily, as he returned to his pile of feathers.

Jim and Jan were less forgiving. "That was *so* unfair," said Jim. "Totally out of order. We could have had him, Peregrine, if we'd joined forces."

"That's never going to happen," said Peregrine.

"Why?" chorused Jim and Jan in unison.

Peregrine had his answer ready. "You know what they say?"

"What?" (Again, in unison.)

"Bird's of a feather, stick together." With that, Peregrine slapped his sides with his wings at his (or so *he* thought) excellent joke.

The words were plain enough for the crows. "Come on, Jan," said Jim, taking flight back to the woods. "We know when we're not wanted."

"At last," sighed Peregrine. "Jimbo gets the message. Now I wonder where *is* my Missus? A nice feast of duck always makes me...."

With that, he was gone. Life on Bowling Green

Marsh returned to normal for the summer visitors.

At least until the next time...

~ * * * THE END * * * ~

S'funny. He turned out OK in the end
A genuine tribute to...?

Johnny was a Leicester lad
His folks were worried he'd turn out bad
He liked the girls; he liked to fight
And always came home late at night
No-one really knew him well
He always seemed to give 'em hell
But inside he had a tale to tell
As his story so unfolds...
He left school (or was he pushed?)
Career prospects were Nil, or rushed
A factory job his destiny
Making things for you and me
Life right then wasn't good enough
A working day was hard and tough
But he was made of sterner stuff
As everybody knows...

His father died and he felt so sad
When he was told, "he's was not your Dad"
It broke his heart so he broke the rules
With, "This life's for losers, and for fools"
The cops were on him, so he was framed
Charged with a felony; he was not to blame
But his reputation became his fame.
With, "Guilty, no parole."

The ladies they all worshipped John
Each one felt they were the one
The one he chose to share his life

Said she'd be a mother (to become his wife)
But when he found he'd been misled
A single life he chose instead
He had a fight; he broke his head
He nearly damn-well died

So family helped at every stage
Johnny's health improved with age
His brothers they all played their part
In a new beginning; a brand new start
Soccer was his one true love
With every blessing from the one above
Reminding him what he's so made of
When another stole his heart
A loving wife is the rarest thing
Happiness all the world can bring
But Johnny took another blow
(How he made it we don't know)
Cancer took his world apart
Leaving Johnny with a broken heart
A poisoned arrow, a fatal dart
Shattered all his dreams

Johnny lives with his memories
Just as life takes, just so it leaves
Ways for us to survive the past
In all our sorrows, tears and laughs
Of all these gifts he's had his share
When he needed someone, they were there
But his greatest passion he holds inside
His badge of honour to wear with pride.

~ * * * ~

The Runaway

I was surprised when you left me
But, now that I recall, you did leave me *some* clues.

We were out for a drive, you and I, passing a
neighbour's house,
You were sat – as usual – on the passenger seat of
my pick-up.
You glanced over to the house and to the farm – for
just a little too long, I now realise.

As your gaze fell back onto the road ahead
I could tell you were wondering -
Had I noticed?

We've always enjoyed our times together
So, you deciding to take off left a hole – a void that,
up until now, only you were able to fill.
I should say I *hoped* we both enjoyed our times
together.
I know I did. I guess you didn't. Not as much.
Not so much that you wanted to stay.

It's our walks I recall most vividly, especially in the
winter.
Those were special days.
Neither of us seemed to mind the cold - wrapped up
against the wind, the snow, but not the rain.
Me, with my thermal layer, cotton shirt, woollen
sweater, and long oilskin,
You with your extra thick winter coat, its inner

lining a protection against the wet.

Do you remember that *particular* day, just after
snow
When we ventured a little too far, until late
afternoon?
In the middle of winter, evenings came early,
Not long after what the well-to-do call 'lunch-time'.
We had to get back before dark. Unlike now, then
there were others who would worry about us
...if we were late.
The river is too wide here, I had said, *even though we
can see our cabin on the other side.*
*Our only option is the bridge, but it's half an hour
away.*
You disagreed.
You didn't actual *say* you disagreed. How *could* you?
You merely took off without a thought.
Across the ice.
I knew it would save us an hour.
We'd be home before dark. In minutes.
So I followed.

Your light frame skipped across the fresh ice.
The river flowed slowly underneath the surface,
If you could actually *see* the surface.
Soon you were on the opposite bank – waiting.
Impatient.
I was half way across when the ice broke - falling in.
Soaked.
I could see you were worried.
You paced up and down the bank, unable to help.
It was the cold I feared most, rather than any

drowning,
After all my feet had hit the river bottom.
And safety. But I was chest deep in water.
(The water was surprisingly warmer than the air.)
Breaking more ice, I forced my way across and soon
reached the opposite bank.
You were pleased to see me safe – and showed it.
We made home before dark after all, keen to be
warm - before my wet clothes could take their toll.

It was spring before we took that same route by the
river.
Until then I never knew our walks *registered* with
you,
Not as memories, at least. But they clearly did.
You proved it to me even without my asking, as you
paused at that very same spot.
The spot where I slipped through the ice -
and you didn't.

You skipped down the bank to the water's edge just
as before.
You looked across to the other side.
And remembered.
Or, perhaps, you just wanted a quicker way home.
If I could read your thoughts you might be saying,
*You waded across before, why not today? And, this
time, you could carry me.*
I could; but I wouldn't; so I didn't.

Evenings, too, were special times we shared.
Again, particularly in the winter.
The shorter days for chores, hunting, collecting

firewood meant longer nights for resting, reading, and reflection.

The warmth of the fire was matched by the warmth of thought for each other – since we faced life here alone, just we two.

So, to see you just leave - like that - was a surprise as well as a disappointment, given the bond we had.
At least I know *where* you are, and *who* you have gone to.

I am also thankful that you waited for the days to lengthen before you made your escape.
If that's what it was. An escape.
The slam of the screen door told me *when* you left.
Looking out the window I saw the direction you took.

Later, as I stood on top of the hillside overlooking our cabin - now *my* cabin - I could trace your steps.
Unfaltering, you made your way to your ultimate destination.
To our neighbour's farm.
Then it came to me. Of course.
You were *his* companion before you became mine.
It was a much larger farm. You had sisters there.
Brothers.
It was those same siblings you had spotted that day.
Yours, on the day we happened to be passing the farm, having missed our turning and taken a different route.

I only have myself to blame.

But at least now I understand.
You were so young when you left him, and them.
Left them for me.
But the pangs of loss and the need for you to return
stayed with you.
But it doesn't help *me* to come to terms with *my* loss.

I miss you more than I could ever make you
understand but it has left me with one most
powerful resolve:

I will never trust another Border collie.

~ * * * ~

Afterword

Thank you for reading my selection of poems and
short stories. I hope you have been entertained by
them and even given you something to think about.

In the next few pages there is information about me
(the author) and some of my other published works
available as e-books and printed copies, on Amazon.

Best wishes
John Morey

About John Morey

John was born in the Leicestershire village of Blaby, to the background of 1950's rock 'n' roll and 1960's Beatlemania, then flower power. Although never part of hippie culture, he was influenced by its sentiments, freedom, and opportunity, now reflected in his writing.

John studied hard to forge a successful career in marketing and publishing, but it was not until he was in his '70s - after marketing 1,000's of books by other authors, in countless genres - he began to write, at the insistence of his wife and encouraged by close friends.

His emotional insights into relationships flavour many of the characters and the actions they take, although none of the works are autobio-graphical – merely drawn on experience.

Visit www.**newnovel.co.uk** for more of John's writing as well as valuable 'how to' articles to help aspiring writers discover the delights of self-publishing.

About 'Love should never be this hard'

Each of the four books in the series chronicles the fortunes of a fictional Romani family mixed with a more conventional culture.

Lives inter-twine and interact from the mid-to-late-1800's right up to the start of the 1970's. Where relevant, real historical context is introduced.

From early beginnings in Southern Ireland there is a migration to and from England, thereafter the background to the novels develops from Cornwall to Devon, and on to the Leicestershire countryside and the village of Blaby - where much of it is set.

On the way there are episodes taking place in Tavistock, short excursions in St Ives and Exmouth, before events finally unfold between Teignmouth and Plymouth - by which time 100 years fly by.

The depiction of life in these locations has already struck a chord with, and approval from, readers familiar with certain locations, justifiably so, as John draws on personal experience in his descriptions.

Each has messages of hope rewarded by perseverance.

The Sign of the Rose (Book 1)

The novels have been called 'an easy read' where historical, location and factual elements entertain as well as inform. They enrich and breathe life into the plot. Characters are believable, even though the story explores the mysteries of the unknown to stretch the imagination.

Leicestershire readers enjoyed experiencing the plot location in 'old Aylestone', Glen Parva and Blaby/Wigston, whereas those familiar with Devon will enjoy the journey across Dartmoor taken by Sean and Rosalee after leaving family behind in Southern Ireland.

But it is in Blaby where the Romani family –

central to all four novels - set down roots, whilst integrating into mainstream society in an ever-changing world.

Within this first book in the series we are introduced to the mystical qualities intrinsic within characters and events, but they remain benign influences, not over-powering the reality and credibility surrounding the basic concepts of this fascinating tale.

If you are a romantic at heart, ready for mixing tragedy with good for-tune, and appreciate love and emotion treated with sensitivity, then the series 'Love should never be this hard' – and this novel - is for you.

The Black Rose of Blaby (Book 2)

Myth - was there really a black rose cultivated in Blaby?

Legend - if the dancing maidens did exist - where is the site of the standing stones now?

Reality - if what they say is true, did the Leicestershire village of Blaby really feed England with a rare treat during WW2?

Lost love - Mary Alice Baker Sercombe graces the cover of this novel. What was the truth behind her ancestors' love affairs?

Myth, legend - reality? You never know the truth with John. That's what makes them intriguing reads.

Many locations actually exist - or used to, captured here for austerity. Characters enjoy a life of their own, often 'composites' of the several people who actually lived. These features add credibility to what are, after all, enjoyable works of fiction.

Beyond that, however, you will relish the escapism built into the plot and sub-plots, right to the final page where an unexpected twist or celebration of the tale holds you to the end.

The story majors on the post-war years up until the start of the 1960's but unearths much of the mysterious past surrounding the events emerging after the dramatic end to Book 1.

Rose: The Missing Years (Book 3)

Readers who know Blaby and surrounding Leicestershire villages particularly enjoyed the reminder of how the old village used to be.

'Rose: The Missing Years' covers the same period as 'Finding Rose', but goes behind the scenes to when she disappears from John's life to take up with Sean, and to have her daughter, Mathilda (Tilly).

Set predominantly in Leicestershire and specifically the village of Blaby, you will find references to its rich heritage and history, much of which is either forgotten or has never been recorded elsewhere.

Nevertheless, like 'Finding Rose', it remains a work of romantic fiction with a thread of mysticism throughout, embedded within imagined Romani culture. An entertaining romantic read, the book also serves as a fascinating social record of the rapidly disappearing country life within a definitive Midlands county.

As with all the novels in the series locations may be real but fictionalised, as are the characters introduced in cameo roles. In similar fash-ion, historic occurrences breathe reality into the fantasy - providing an element of grounding to the plot - but dates may be 'stretched'.

For maximum effect, read Books 3 and 4 in quick succession.

Finding Rose (Book 4)

The location of the story begins in Blaby before switching between Plymouth and Teignmouth - recounting events set some fifty years ago - with a brief episode in St Ives, Cornwall.

Romantic mysticism enters the lives of more people than we may care to admit. It does here, but without the trappings of horror or menace. Rose and John are, themselves, a benign force and, although their journey is not without sadness and heartache, their perseverance towards fulfilment remains undaunted.

Discover two people on a journey without knowing how, where, or with whom it will end. Will they survive as one? or apart? And what did happen in Rose's life in the seven 'missing years'?

Answers were in the previous book but this fascinating read will take you a little further, leaving you with a feeling that 'some things do end happily after all'.

Supplement to the collection of short stories and poems
Memoir of a Blaby Boy: 1950-1970

Foreword

The following narrative represents the author's selective memory from his early days immediately after World War Two until he forsook his birthplace of Blaby, Leicestershire for the West Country.

It is largely true, whilst allowing a degree of exaggeration and fact-switching for (hopefully) dramatic effect or to massage the author's recollection of what really might have happened.

The style may – in parts – become over-indulgent, for which the author apologises. However, for those keen to recall or understand for the first time what life in a small English village was like in the period covered, what follows should deliver.

Students of local history and social change – whether from the Midlands or further afield – may also find this 'record' of real value.

These are the author's honest motives, born from a disappointment in the way that his native Blaby has changed – some would say for the worst – from the day he left in 1970.

This account begins with the author, John Morey, at four years old, living with his parents and three siblings in a modest bungalow on The Avenue, Blaby.

THE CHANGING YEARS
Reflection on a life no more

There's nothing new in saying that we are a product of our environment; the child being the father of the man and all that.

Being born soon after WW2 may not have seemed like a privilege at the time – a time of austerity, doing without and "making do" - but for me it was. There was always the living in fear bit, fear that the terrors of war could easily return, as stories of true horror were still fresh in the memory and part of daily conversation among adults.

When you're only five years old it's bound to make an impression. *The whole world does.*

In reality, only adults experienced and shared these accounts in any detail. Nevertheless, they still managed to permeate down as a general mood, affecting all ages and influencing lives across all generations. Including my own. Detail is lost anyway, when you are too young to understand the context and the 'reference points' as we now know them.

Such was the background to my early years and to those of my family. It shaped our attitudes and values. It was a time of change – more so for our parents, who had a status quo ready to be affected. In our own early school days, we had very little you could call 'established' that was ready for change.

But the changes that were in progress included

both the material and the spiritual, the negative as well as the positive occurrences in our daily lives, affecting our views on class, religion, patriotism, career aspirations, the place of women in society, our place in society and the world, our relationships with our neighbours, bosses, within our community as well as within our own family. And so on...

The one thing it did not change was the ability and willingness of countries to go to war.

Seventy years on and well into the twenty first century war is as real, threatening, devastating and immoral as it ever was.

MY FAMILY
Growing up in 1950s Leicestershire

I loved my parents so much, even in my early 20's I could not imagine life without them.

They had me late in their lives, so mortality was closer for them than it was for the parents of other children I knew. They were the foundation for the love and caring within our family and present every second of the day with such power that it infused the values of my brother and sisters. I would like to think that some of it rubbed off on me too.

And it was indelible.

Both parents worked hard. Mam (the Midlands word for 'Mum' or 'Mother') was semi-skilled as a factory machinist. She took in assembly work for the hosiery and boot and shoe factories, working as a home-worker – a popular option after the war for those with pre-school children.

She was not the sort to sit down and read a book, there was no TV at that time. Nor did she bother with women's social groups. Instead, when she was not earning a living, she would be saving money by darning socks or knitting clothes for us to wear. Or taking a well-deserved nap.

I used to complain when she made me hold my arms out to hold a skein of wool so that she could turn it into a ball, ready to knit. Despite that, I can still picture the roasting fire that seemed to be always 'in' during cold winter days and nights. We would be sat as close as we could without being scorched until the last skein was finished.

The other 'special treat' was that, because Mam was at home and both Brian and Betty (siblings) would be at school, I had her all to myself. This made me somewhat possessive and dependant on her (which I talk about a little later on). But it left me with an impression that everything around me was warm – and safe.

Although clearly untrue and a stretch of my nostalgic imagination, every day *seemed* to be warm and sunny. The house was always warm thanks to that roaring open fire. It doubled as a means to dry clothes in the winter, or to make toast by holding a slice of bread in front of it with a brass toasting fork.

I don't recall much about Dad at that time, apart from the feeling that he was always cross with me. He would shout and, when I was a little older, give me a clout if I deserved it. He would later say that "I was a mistake" and that he would "put me in a home" if I misbehaved. It was perhaps thirty years after those early days before I knew he didn't really mean it. In fact, he had become proud of what I had become as I made my own way in life.

Times just after the war were hard for the family, so I suppose he never meant to come over as strict, let alone unkind and, most certainly, not cruel. I was his safety valve. Apparently he was a travelling representative for Singer sewing machines, which is why he never seemed to be around except at weekends, often coming home after I had gone to bed.

It also explains how we came to have a Singer sewing machine enabling Mam to earn valuable housekeeping to support four children.

Brian was seven years older than me and I have no recollection of him in those early years. We must have shared a bedroom. My sisters, Joan and Betty, shared a room. I must also have gone on to share his clothes when he outgrew them – a common feature of family life in those days, "hand-me-downs".

Betty was five years older than Brian and won a scholarship to Lutterworth Grammar School. That meant a long school day for her. Lutterworth was eight miles away, to which she probably travelled on a school bus, unless Dad was able to take her in his Singer company car. We regarded Betty as 'posh' and not in the same working class category as we were. She even spoke differently, pronouncing her words differently and using words we had not even heard.

Needless to say, other than an impression I recall nothing of Betty from those early years pre-school and later – not until I was at secondary school age. Except one vague memory. It must have been in her summer term and the school had an open day, or a sports day. Apart from Joan, who worked then, we arrived to a field on a lovely summer's day, a festival bedecked with white marquees, and tents, bunting and flags. It was the Lutterworth Grammar School sports day or show. I think I even recall a Gymkhana (as I later determined it must have been) as the main attraction in the centre of the field. That's how 'upper crust' her kind of school life was.

At the other end of the scale, sister Joan was five years older than Betty, and worked at Griffin & Gamble in their factory, I believe it was as a machinist who worked fast and earned quite good money.

Looking back, and in context, that made sense. Women had been liberated by the war when they had to step into men's shoes and do men's jobs. (My aunt Rowena even drove a bread van in the war.)

Those years of austerity left people like my sister with an urgency to make hay while the sun shone, to appreciate employment opportunities, and to earn the money if it was there to be earned. Plus – unlike the generation that followed her, she saved for the good things in life she wanted, rather than become victim of hire purchase (the 'never-never') and, much later, the credit card culture.

We were fortunate to live in a household of over-whelming love for each other. Ironically we never said out loud that we loved each other, and never kissed each other hello or goodbye. That was for softies or for posh people. (That said, I think Betty caught that social habit due to influences from grammar school.)

Mam and Dad would exchange kisses when Dad went off to work, otherwise neither ever told any of us that they loved us, nor did any of we children tell each other we loved each other. But we did. All of us.

For us, love manifested itself when it was required, when the occasion presented itself. As a small boy, sister Betty would comfort me if she felt that Dad had shouted at me unfairly; even as a teenager, I would get the occasional pomegranate (yes!) from Joan on a Saturday, which I loved.

No big deal, you may say, but these small kindnesses spoke volumes then, as they still do, now.

Dad was strict, but I always appreciated his encouragement if I did well at school; Mam was always kind and this instance I am about to reveal was typical of the sacrifices she made for me out of love.

It was just before the new school term. I must have been about 13 years old – the age when you become self-conscious about your appearance. You need to impress.

I needed a new top coat for the winter. The norm was to have a gabardine raincoat and put on an extra layer, but I saw this raglan-sleeved light brown coat in the shop window just as we were giving up hope of finding a coat that fitted me, and at the right price.

The problem was that it was half as expensive again as the raincoat.

Mam explained this but I, selfishly, was insistent that I wanted the alternative I had seen in the window. It was late Saturday afternoon, in Leicester, and getting dark. I can still see it all now.

I must have stayed *outside* the shop, peering in as Mam explained things to the shop assistant. What these 'things' were I could only guess. Afterwards, it transpired that they worked out a price that was below the ticket price, was more than she strictly "could afford", but left her with just enough – *just* enough – for our bus fare home.

Eventually I was called in out of the cold (it was after four in the afternoon in winter, and dark) to try on the coat to ensure it fitted. It didn't. Not properly, anyway. It was a tad too long at the sleeves and across the chest. But I still wanted it, so I was delighted when Mam assured us all that 'he'll grow into it". I was determined I would.

At the time I was delighted, of course. However, years later and even now, I fill up with love for my Mam for the way she placed *my* needs, my *selfish* needs, above all else, and the sacrifices she must have had to make – finding money from somewhere else, or 'doing without', just for my benefit.

I think the term is 'unconditional love'.

THE CHILDHOOD
First - The Avenue, Blaby

Playing in the gutter as a much sought-after pastime is not as bad as it sounds.

In those days – I guess I am talking about 1949 – the village streets were pretty much devoid of cars. Streets and pavements were clean, if you ignore the odd dollop of horse manure in the road after the milkman had made his deliveries.

So, too, were the gutters clean. People kept them that way, and by "people" I meant those who lived in our street – as well as the regular road sweeper, a man with a brush, not a vehicle. Not that I always welcomed the road-sweeper. He took away the "sand" in the gutter that I used to dam the stream of water after a sudden shower.

The street ,as I call it, was in fact "The Avenue". Literally. It had trees on both sides, growing out of the pavements. And we lived in a small bungalow half way up the street (or half way down, depending on which way you were going). It really an avenue, as I said, lined with trees, but I am not sure what sort. All I remember was that they were not the sort you could climb as their branches started way up the trunk, and certainly out of reach for a four year old. But always, always, there were pigeons cooing on a warm summer's afternoon.

So, you may ask, how come this small child was playing in the gutter, on his own, in a mostly empty street? Wasn't his mother worried he might get run over, or kidnapped, or worse? The truth was that, at that age – pre-school – you hadn't got into the "making friends" bit, so you played on your own, although there *was* this other boy called Dave Freeman living in one of the big houses opposite.

The other reason was because my brother was seven years older. Brian was either at school during the day or, at weekends, playing with *his* friends. Usually Sammy Wale or Colin Swanwick. My two sisters were even older, old enough to go to work.

Dad worked too. Which is why I hardly saw him. Mam was a "home-worker" (I discovered later). That meant that she had a sewing machine in the kitchen and made things – at home. Geddit?

So.

That's how I came to be playing out in the street, on my own, building dams for the stream of water in the gutter after a sudden shower. I had boats, too.

OK, let's call them sticks.

And before you ask, "Why didn't you have real toy boats?", as I just explained, this was 1949, after the war. The austere years. No money for toys, unless it was Christmas. Not much money for clothes either, which is why I was probably wearing the shirt and trousers Brian had out-grown 4-5 years earlier.

One other thing about toys. Toy battleships – the kind you might think to play with in the bath as a small boy. They were made of lead! Yes. They sank! I never did get that bit. And, just to illustrate how attitudes have changed, back then we were concerned that the ships would not float; nowadays 'they' (the authorities) would be more worried we would go down with lead poisoning.

Now, in the 21st Century, for so many reasons children of my age would not be playing in the street on their own. For one thing it would not be considered safe. Then it was – safe from traffic, other kids wanting to do you damage, and from other adults wanting to do much worse.

Not that I was neglected hours on end. I am sure Mam was either in the front garden, or looking out of the window as she darned our socks. (If you don't know what that means, Google it!)

Yes we had a front garden – as well as a back garden with fruit trees, a shed, and a lawn – backing onto an allotment where we grew even more fruit, vegetables, chickens... you get the picture.

The front garden was just a few feet of lawn, bordered by a privet hedge (I once found a Dad cat under it), and a gate opening onto the pavement. So I was safe. Satisfied?

Next door lived Mr and Mrs Meyer. I guess they were German Jews. Refugees from the war? They had more money than we did because Mr Meyer was an optician. Don't ask me how I worked that out at 3-4 years old. The main point about mentioning the Meyers was that Mrs Meyer used to give me sweets using their ration book. (Again, Google that if you are unsure....) I remember my Mam thanking her for her kindness. (I wasn't allowed to take the sweets *direct* from Mrs Meyer.)

So what else does a four year old remember?

I was afraid of my Dad. Why did I annoy him so much? Why did he always have to shout at me? I guess I misbehaved – but how? And why almost all the time?

He took that to his grave. I never asked, not even in later life. Funny thing is, I was hardly aware of Brian, or sisters Betty and Joan. They didn't impact on my daily life, probably because they had just discovered boys. That could have caused a bit of friction for Dad.

But 'what about Brian?' I hear you ask.

Oh, he was perfect, and never did anything wrong. Shall we move on...?

I did not start school until I was five. I suppose then I made my first friends – Melv, but, first, Dave Freeman from across the street.

Dave had two elder brothers and a sister. That bit I do remember. And he did not have a Dad – or he was away a lot. Their house was bigger than ours, and I recall Mrs Freeman being a bit posh.

Sometimes I would go over there to play, which I loved. I had two big reasons for going over:

One, he had a rocking horse.

Two, they had a TV. (They must have been seriously loaded.)

After school we would watch Bill & Ben, Children of The New Forest, and I suppose The Cisco Kid. Oh, and Andy Pandy!

Dave and I remained friends until he won a secondary school scholarship for Loughborough Art College as a boarder. Later, the family emigrated to Canada.

OK, so now I must be five years old. Any more memories to share?

My eldest sister, Joan, was "courting" her future husband, Derek. He came from a council house family and was an absolute diamond in every way. Initially, my Dad did not approve of this beau from the wrong side of the tracks but they became almost like brothers. Not only that, but Derek became a second Dad to me, even though, at five years old, I seemed to always annoy him, too! (I wouldn't let him read my comics, if you really want to know the truth.)

My earliest recollection was to hear his motorbike – apparently a mile or so down the road – as he came to pick up Joan. I can see Joan even now, in front of the mirror in Mam and Dad's bedroom, getting ready to go out – hurrying as she heard to the familiar "pop-pop" of Derek's bike.

Betty was five years younger than Joan. As I explained earlier, she went to Grammar School in Lutterworth on a scholarship, and was also a Sunday School teacher. She was a gentler spirit and her superior education had made her posh. You could tell by the way she talked. Joan, on the other hand, worked at Griffin and Gamble, in the factory round the corner from where we lived – in Park Road.

I can still see Betty now, having been walked home from Sunday School by a chap called Derek Smith (?) standing one side of the gate, with him on the other. Betty was telling me to go away. But why? Then he stopped calling.

I found out later – when I could understand what it meant – he went to The Congo as a missionary.

This was at the time the Mau Mau were killing people. Betty was asked to go with him but refused. (Ironically, years later when Betty was in her thirties, she met a second generation white South African, married him and settled over there.)

I START SCHOOL

Now we come to Miss Shields. She was my first primary school teacher and was gorgeous. I was unaware who the film actress Rhonda Fleming was at this point, but that is who Miss Shields resembled. Slim, blonde – and posh enough to own an open-top sports car. Probably a Morgan.

One thing I recall. She picked up my Mam one day to take her to vote in the national election. Yes, the sports car was red. Yes, they drove off with the hood down. Mam wore a head-scarf.

As ever, Mam wore a top coat (even though it was perhaps May) – plus a handbag. One thing about handbags in those days, they had a centre clasp – on the top, not the side, and it "snapped" as you closed it. I loved to open and close it. For long periods of time. That may explain why I could be so annoying to my Dad. He was usually in the room!

As you can imagine, after so many years the events, but more especially the order they came in, tend to blur. So I am now going into an "in no particular order" time frame.

Miss Shields was such a lovely person – and perfect for her vocation. Soon after I started primary school we had a new Head Teacher, Mr. Dixon. He took over from Mr Backhouse, who had stayed so long he had taught both my older sisters.

If you are still alive, Mr. D, I don't actually blame you for what I am about to say, but you did have an early, negative, affect on my confidence level.

Dr Barnardo's was a charity supporting disadvantaged children. One day, everyone in the school was given an envelope to take home and collect whatever their parents could afford to donate. I gave in my envelope, which was kept anonymous. A day or two later Mr. Dixon entered the classroom to address us. For whatever reason we were all sat on the floor at the time.

He explained that it had come to his notice that some children spent their donation on sweets. He then invited anyone guilty of this to raise their hand. As I said, we were sat on the floor. However, I had my arm resting on the desk *above* me, *looking* as if I had my hand raised. But I wasn't.

Mr. Dixon picked me out and then proceeded to ask me why I had committed this heinous crime. I hadn't done anything wrong but, somehow, I was so intimidated that I was unable to deny it or speak in my defence. I think I must have muttered, 'I don't know' which, as any lawyer will confirm, is an admission of guilt.

At least it is if your accuser is the Headmaster and you are just five years old. Although no action was taken against me the damage was done. I was shamed in front of the whole school. I never forgot it – that feeling of an innocent wrongly condemned.

A little later, after Mr. Dixon had left the room, Miss Shields knelt down next to me, me sitting in my tiny desk, to ask me why I had done it.

Only then was I able to say that I hadn't taken the money, and explained that I was too frightened to say so. (Yes, in those days you respected your teachers without question.) Miss Shields cleared my name with the Headmaster but the experience left me scarred, probably to this day. I very often, quite wrongly, feel that I am being accused when I am not. It's a hang-up I live with.

I went to the village school, Blaby C of E. As I said, so did both my sisters. Mr. Backhouse was Headmaster then, and for just one term when I started. By that time he was ancient. Over 20 years had passed.

Easily six foot in height, he was thin and angular and rode a big bicycle. Even so, he looked too big for it. One thing that changed when he left was that they eventually took out the open fireplace – that was a lovely sight on a cold and frosty winter's day – to put in a new boiler and extra radiators. Luckily, I was able to enjoy several years of its warmth before progress – and central heating – took over.

Another teacher who left soon after was a career spinster teacher called Miss Basham. Yes, she had a deep voice and wore sensible shoes. Yes, that *was* her real name! But she was very kind, and because she was a strong character we felt safe on our nature walks.

Unlike the rest of the family, Brian went to Whetstone Primary – the school in the next village. However, it was no further than where we lived in The Avenue because Mam and Brian were able to

walk across three farmland fields, on a footpath**
behind us.

It was not until much later that I questioned Mam
as to why I did not go to Whetstone.

"Well, I didn't want Brian to have to cross the
busy Lutterworth Road to the Blaby school." was her
reply. (Marvellous!)

"OK," I thought, "so whilst it's *not OK* for Brian to
risk life and limb crossing the main road, *it is OK* for
me to get squashed?" Jeez. Was I playing the victim
again? And had Dad been honest all along about my
being a mistake?

I mentioned that Brian had two friends in
particular, Sammy Wale and Colin Swanwick, who
both lived in The Avenue. Like Betty, Brian did not
want little brother intruding on his social life.

On one occasion, Brian relented. So I tagged
along on one of his rambles across nearby fields.
Apparently there was a circus nearby at the time.
They had elephants. To this day – but very rarely, I
admit – I dream of that walk. Now, whether it's true,
or part of the dream, on the ramble we came across
elephant footprints. Nah! Just cannot be true!

** *Much, much later, I was part of a Blaby gang of
kids (aged say 10 to 15) who went to war with a
group of similar ruffians from Whetstone. It was
about the ownership of the field in the middle of the
one that was clearly ours, and the one closest to
Whetstone.*

*Each gang assembled at the gates at either end of
the field in the middle – and threw bricks and stones
at each other. Amazing! We could have been killed.
Luckily, nobody was hurt. Nobody won, nobody lost,*

we just got tired after a while and went home.

Back to the main plot...

Two other instances that occurred, but without me knowing about it, I still remember from stories.

The first happened in the local sweet shop owned by Mabel Pegg. (Yes, all she sold were sweets, usually taking ration book tokens.) Her shop was a converted house on Enderby Road, with sweet jars adorning her front bay window.

It involved my Mam taking my sister Joan for a treat – only to encounter her first Chinaman! She screamed the place down. You see, it's not remarkable in itself, apart from highlighting the fact that then – in the 1940's – most people in those days so insular, rarely exposed to anything outside of the immediate vicinity. There was radio, but no TV, so other cultures rarely featured – visually at least.

The second happened when I swallowed a sugared almond, probably bought from Mabel Pegg's – which stuck in my throat. I stopped breathing. I was turning blue. No phone. No doctor nearby. All Dad could think of doing was to pick me up and run for the nearest surgery – easily a mile away. I can only guess he didn't have a car at the time.

Luckily he only made less than that before he tired – and fell over with me in his arms. The jolt dislodged the sweet and saved my life.

HILLVIEW NURSERIES – on Lutterworth Road

First of all let's get one thing straight, **my Dad**

founded Hillview Nurseries back in the 1950's.
For the record, it was NOT started by the
grandparent's of a liberal democrat politician.

Before Dad christened his smallholding 'Hillview
Nurseries' I remember my Mam taking me up there
on several occasions, from where we lived at the
time in The Avenue. Situated opposite Blaby Rose
Gardens, it was out of the village along the
Lutterworth Road. Quite a trek, although I was
probably still in a pushchair – so it was doubly hard
for Mam.

Even so, Mam walked up to join Dad as he toiled
in the fields, bringing welcome refreshments. These
usually consisted of sandwiches and a bottle of tea.
Thermos flasks were expensive. We made do with a
lemonade bottle filled with hot tea – without
cracking the glass – and wrapped it in a towel to
keep it hot until we arrived after half an hour walk.

We had just the one dog at the time. A long-
haired black & white collie cross called Bob. We all
loved him. He became my dog later on until he died
aged 13 years. I can still recall him panting in the
summer heat. At the end of his life, one day he just
took himself off to lay in the ditch opposite our
house (by then we had moved back into the village),
where he died. Dad never could understand why he
decided to look under that ditch when he first
realised he was missing.

Out at 'the field' as we called it, before we built a
bungalow and actually lived there, occasionally in
those early days we were caught in a thunder storm.
There were no shelters, so we snuggled under the
thick hawthorn hedgerow. At the time, crops of

cabbages, peas, Brussel sprouts and cauliflower were harvested in jute "sack bags". From those the contents were transferred into bushel boxes for market.

But sack bags were useful for many things.

We made capes out of them by tucking one corner into its opposite to make a hood, which we draped over our head. They were almost waterproof! Hedgerows provided the rest of the shelter.

Another use for sack bags, I found out later, was when we had a young border collie bitch for Bob. Bess was short-haired, and she suffered from fits. Dad knew the answer. Not tablets.

Bess would "fit" and run and run around the 10-acre smallholding until she simply just got tired. Then Dad would catch her and, still fitting, she would be put into a sack bag and kept quiet. After a while she would be fine. Dad's natural sense of love and caring came out on occasions just like that. Eventually, Bess stopped having fits and went on to give us two litters of pups.

To this day I remember her pups – first a litter of seven, then the second time six – running round the garden after me. I also recall Dad saying not to disturb Bess when she was at the point of giving birth – in a dark airing cupboard – in case she ate them!

We sold them – dogs were twenty one shillings (about one pound or a dollar fifty each), bitches a little less at eighteen shillings and sixpence. I was sad to see them go, but we needed the money, not more dog mouths to feed.

Bess also became *my* dog and faithful companion until she died too at age 13. Hit by a lorry.

Dad wanted to build a house on our smallholding so that we could leave The Avenue and live there, with Hillview Nurseries a full-time business. But the planners didn't want it.

A Blaby by-pass was on the planning department's forward plans – one route of which was for it to cross our 10-acre nursery. This placed a restriction on Dad being able to build a home for us on the site. He fought and eventually managed to build a bungalow on the far corner of the land, furthest away from the main Lutterworth Road.

The earliest recollection of our new home was when we moved in without gas and perhaps even electric. I vividly recall Mam cooking on an open fire – in what was to become our back garden!

Yes – we must have pioneered the outdoor barbecue in the UK.

This must have been 1950. All four children were still living at home. Joan now had to walk, I guess, the mile or so to the factory in the village where we used to live. But not to worry. She must have married Derek not long after and moved to Aylestone, and a new job.

Betty was also working, at just 16 years old. She had started out as a dressmaker, I think in Leicester – but it did not work out. To this day I remember Mam and Dad consoling her when she came home one day, apparently having been "let go".

Unconditional love like that stayed with me.

That's how Betty became a shorthand-typist and then secretary – at English Electric – where, not until she was in her thirties, did she meet and married Denys, who was on secondment from South Africa.

Anyway, back to the then present, Betty thrived in the secretarial and management environment. It was originally called Power Jets. Sir Frank Whittle developed the jet engine there in WW2 before, disenchanted by the way the government, he was enticed to take an offer from the USA military .

I mention that because we could still hear the turbines being tested even after Frank had left (!). The factory was only a mile and a half away, across (Farmer) Bert Atfield's land which, itself, stretched into neighbouring Whetstone.

Our modest three-bedroom bungalow was quiet and cosy, with Joan and Betty sharing a room, as did Brian and me – but later Joan left to marry Derek. I remember nothing of their wedding.

What I do recall, however, was that I was a very clinging child – to my Mam. "Mardy" was the local dialectic term for my unreasonable behaviour. How do I know? My oldest sister told me! Several times.

Within a 10-minute walking distance from Hillview Nurseries was the Dog and Gun pub, next door to the British Road Services depot. Mam and Dad liked to go to the pub occasionally.

That's when I would always kick off – screaming and crying and generally being a pain in the neck for my sisters and brother, until Mam and Dad returned. I was pathetic.

I had the usual childhood illnesses, like measles, soon after the move. I had already got over whooping cough apparently. Apart from that I did not have chicken pox until I was in my forties!

The reason I mention this is two-fold:

One, I remember the taste of the medicine – which was not half bad;

Two, the doctor made home visits – certainly unheard of nowadays. The National Health Service was in its infancy. Efficient and solvent!

Running Hillview Nurseries was hard work for both Mam and Dad. It was also unprofitable, mainly due to cruel summers and harsh winters. So much so that Mam took a job in a local hosiery factory – she had to. Dad became the local postman – he had to. The latter was convenient as the early hours – start and finish – suited him because he could still work in the field after his shift. Eventually, of course, this took its toll and we sold up and moved back into the village.

I think we lived on the nursery from 1950 to 1954. I do recall that we sold it to Estonian refugees (who were fleeing a hostile Soviet regime). The daughter of the family was about my age. I vaguely remember her. It was she who got it wrong in an article in The Leicester Mercury saying that her parents had *started* the nursery. In fact they only took it over as a going concern. Her son became a politician – so perhaps that could explain why the facts were distorted somewhat.

All our family pitched in with the job of raising crops and harvesting. These included brassicas, berry fruits, a salad garden, potatoes and other vegetables, peas and beans, as well as keeping poultry.

We were usually employed "thinning out" as the crops were reaching maturity and then ultimately picking ready for market. Brussel sprouts were the worst – in February with the frost still on them. Dad also took on university students on a day-to-day basis at pea-picking time.

Just one point on this. It really makes me sad that, currently, vegetable growers are complaining that they cannot get enough (foreign, Eastern European) workers to gather in and process the crops. Where are all the students? Too proud for such labour?

Back then there were a mere 3% of school leavers who qualified for university; now we aspire to 50%. Surely that means a massively inflated number of available workers now available after university term has finished. Or is the work considered beneath them? Sad!

Back then there were also 'professional' farm labourers, albeit casual, including a Mr. Toone ("Tooney") and Mr. Paramour. These were your typical agricultural labourers from the village. Both use to arrive together, by bike, which was really comical in a way as Mr. Paramour was about half as tall again as Tooney. I enjoyed this contact with adults outside of the family, but they rarely stopped to talk to me and just got on with their work.

David Thomas was different, though, being younger (in his teens?), and apparently not so hard-working according to Dad. He was easily distracted by a pestering 5-year-old. He didn't last long.

Brian was coming up to school-leaving age and helped Dad enormously because he drove the tractor – a Fordson Major. It was temperamental and stalled every few minutes. Finally we found out it was a blocked filter. Farmer Rest in the village apparently diagnosed this for Dad.

Dad let me sit on the back of the harrow for extra weight (!), that I do know. I felt I was contributing.

Another tractor in the lives of Brian and me was a little Ferguson, owned by Blaby Rose Gardens run by Dutch people – Mr Beschovel was the owner assisted by his manager, Mr Hanraads. Beschovel did not like Dad: first because he would not sell the land to him; second because Dad let some sections go fallow some years and Beschovel didn't like the weeds seeding amongst his rose crops.

Mr Hanraads was lovely, and let us sit on his tractor while he took a photograph of Brian and me. This I still have. He and his wife stayed friends with us long after we left Hillview Nurseries and he eventually set up on his own, helped by his sons.

As I said, Brian was about to start work, so his help for Dad was evenings and weekends. The job he took was at – guess where – English Electric. Brian went to South Wigston Secondary Modern school where his best subject seemed to be Technical Drawing. No surprise then that he was taken on as an Apprentice Draftsman. (Later I went to the same school, with the same teachers, by which time it was rebadged a High School.)

Two things come to mind: sister Betty already worked at the English Electric and cycled to work on a yellow and black, drop-handle-bar Dawes Domino

(I think); so did Brian, exactly the same model and colour – but a man's bike, probably bought on hire-purchase; second, he got it stolen when he left it outside of Sammy Wale's house when they went to the cinema (The Plaza); also of note is that Mam went with Brian for his interview at English Electric. (And they said I was spoilt!)

OK, so that's three, but I was never good at maths then, and I guess he had to be accompanied by Mam because a minor was not allowed to sign an apprenticeship contract.

Overall I remember the days at Hillview Nurseries with a great deal of fondness, even though no friends from school ever made it the mile or so out of the village to play. One exception was Adrian ("Age") Meredith who came out one time on my birthday. I made him jam sandwiches because my Mam was still at work and Dad was out in the field.

The big event, though, and one I was never allowed to forget was the time I set the Christmas tree on fire! (Later, even as a teenager I rarely took a girl home but I was always reminded – usually by my sister Joan – with, "Did he tell about when he set the Christmas tree on fire?". How embarrassing!)

Here's what actually happened.

Dad and Brian were working in the field. At that time it got dark about 4 o'clock and Brian must have been on a break from school. Mam was at work in a factory in the village – about a mile away. It was still light and I had been reading a comic showing a tree decorated with candles. Ours was decked in cotton wool to simulate snow. The open fire was roaring away. I folded up some newspaper, lit it, putting it to one of the pieces of cotton wool. I felt so safe.

Until it all went up in flames. Terrified, I opened up the French doors and ran outside shouting, "The Christmas tree's on fire! The Christmas tree's on fire!". Brian and Dad ran up to the house. I ran off to hide in the tall cabbages. Bess, my faithful collie-cross, followed me. (Tail wagging!)

I waited there in the December chill without a coat, huddled to Bess for warmth. I had seen Dad put out the fire, smoke billowing from the open windows in the lounge. It must have been an hour at least before I picked out Mam in the dark, as she turned into our driveway, on her way home from work. What she must have thought!

I ran from my hiding in the cabbages, explaining to her what had happened and, of course, that "I didn't mean to do it". In we went to the warmth of the kitchen, with Brian and Dad waiting for me.

Usually, Dad would "give me a clout" if I misbehaved - "boxing my ears" as they would say. This time he didn't. He sat there silently, reading the daily local paper. But there was a punishment. Even today I find it amusing.

In those days, everyone had a local newspaper delivered. The Leicester Mercury ran a comic strip that I followed every day – *Ronnie Raindrop*. My punishment was that I was not allowed to read *Ronnie Raindrop* for the next few days.

Who says the punishment doesn't fit the crime? Of course, the real punishment is that none of the family allowed me to 'live it down' for years afterwards – until well into my twenties. It was one part of Christmas I always dreaded – the reminder of my misdeed – and we didn't have another Christmas tree for years afterwards.

Anyway, with that out of the way can we please get on with the real issues at hand?

One thing I just cannot understand even today. I said earlier that Hillview Nurseries was a mile or so out of the village where Mam's workplace and my school was.

Occasionally, Dad would take me to school on the cross-bar of his bicycle, (by that I mean I was sat on the cross-bar, not Dad!) which was quite painful, despite the cushion Dad had tied to it. Otherwise, I would have had to walk - on my own – as a 9 year-old – along the pavement of the busy Lutterworth Road. That was the main road from Leicester to London, before the M1 motorway was built.

The ridiculous part of it all was that I used to go home for lunch, rather than take sandwiches or have school dinners. I had to make it home and back in one hour. By special arrangement I was allowed to leave 5 minutes before the other children. Amazing, looking back on it.

Before leaving the era of being a country boy, I must say something about certain other experiences that left an indelible, often fond, impression with me to this day.

Although the nursery was a smallholding in more ways than one, Dad still managed to lay part of it to hay. Without machinery to do the work, Dad scythed the grass by hand, and made into a couple of haystacks, rather than into bales. Small ones, but the smell of newly stacked hay was a delight, as was the heat that exuded from them as you burrowed into their centre. (I think this heat needed to be released anyway to stop it catching fire.)

We had no cattle or horses so the only thing I can guess he needed hay for were the chickens. We ate the eggs, obviously, and on special occasions we would occasionally eat of chicken. They were expensive to buy in those days before battery farms – and that's when you could get them. This was way before supermarkets and frozen food.

69, LUTTERWORTH ROAD, BLABY

In 1954 we moved from Hillview Nurseries to a house built by a local builder, Len Potter. It was a semi-detached three-bedroom house at 69, Lutterworth Road. Len Potter took the other house for his family and we had the local Police House next door to us, on the other side of a jitty between us – it was a public right of way leading to the council houses that were later built behind ours.

Mr Madison was the village policeman. He had a son, a little younger than me, called Roy, who (and I could never get over this fact) had to have a glass of milk every day which his grandmother always insisted he had, which I felt was gross. We even had to sit there, sometimes, while he downed it in one.

You were also not allowed to swear in front of the Madison's – by swear I mean "bugger" and "sod".

The swear words used commonly today – the 'f-word' and worse - were simply not known by children our age, and never used by adults in front of children.

I think the house cost £1,200. Mam and Dad took out a mortgage for it. I did a quick comparison based on the value of the pound in 1954 versus now. The equivalent house price today would be £35,000 – which only goes to show how expensive they are now, compared with then.

We were also able to afford a car. Mam still worked in a factory in the village, whilst Dad took a job in the store room at Midland Hosiery Mills – probably at about £10 a week or £300 a week (£15,000 a year) in today's money. That's not a lot by today's standards but, considering how cheap the houses were, I guess it all levels out.

This 'career move' may have been a step down for Dad. As a young man he was one of the youngest factory foremen at Percival's * in the shoe industry. Dad always maintained an interest in shoes. He sometimes mended his own soles and heels. If we bought a pair of new shoes ourselves, we always showed them to Dad to inspect them when we got home for "quality control".

(*Wind the clock forward fifty years and the ailing Percival's was bought by my best school mate, Mick Charlton, in an attempt to save it from going under. Unfortunately, Mick was not successful. Another casualty would have been another well-known village lad, Pete ('Dusty') Miller, who worked there and was a wonderful character and a great player to have in your soccer team.)

Events that follow may be somewhat random or, at least, out of chronological order. Broadly, though, they will cover my life from age 8 to 11 years old.

The biggest change for me was that I had friends - neighbours' children as well as school friends, who I would play with out of school.

Melvyn Wale was my first long-standing playmate, and we both shared other friends who we grew up with together – some well into our teens. Popular games were "exploring" - usually the fields and hedgerows nearby and making a den – scrumping (stealing apples from local orchards), cowboys and Indians and, pretty soon, soccer.

Melvyn became a very successful local soccer player, scoring hundreds of goals over a long period playing for some 40 years. Initially, though, he didn't get the hang of it and did more damage to other players than to the ball. As an 8 year old that earned him the nick-name "kick-hoss Wale" due to his enthusiasm exceeding his skill level.

Cruel though that may have seemed at the time, it could well have been the making of him. In fact, it may have defined his success for all the years to come as a renowned local sportsman (principally soccer and cricket, but also tennis). Not only that, he excelled in musical performance as lead singer for the Seven Seas band, then later as award winner in local drama as both actor and director. But most of all he was, and is, a perfect role model and father for his and Sue's delightful children and grandchildren.

Underpinning all this was a solid career as a

salesman and, in the few years prior to retirement, a "pied-piper" style sports teacher for the local junior school. This was also matched by commendable leadership qualities applied to sports management – especially in local soccer. Yes. 'The boy did good.'

The main point I am making is that Melv is a prime example of how self-belief can break down so many barriers to success, even overturning early set-backs in childhood. But allow me now, dear reader, to fast-forward a few years to my own achievements on the sports field whilst at school.

They were very few. Only recently have some of "the reasons why" emerged.

Melv and I were both spotted by some of the 'big kids' in the village for their local soccer team. (The term 'big kids' is defined by them being fourteen years old to our nine. It's a comparative term.)

One 'big kid' in particular inspired me by giving me my first pair of soccer boots. They were old-style "Tom Finney type" pure leather with high ankles and studs fixed with nails to the sole. The significance of this is that, as the studs wore down, the nails burst through the insole to spike your feet. Painful! I was size 5 and the boots were size 7 – but I loved them to bits. Pre-worn as they were, I cleaned and applied dubbin to them after every match.

That early success led me to be picked for the junior school team, playing on the wing. I was "OK" (not brilliant), but an ever-present, and scored four goals! Mr Buxton was our teacher and coach. Centre forward Derek Pawley was our best player alongside Dave Freeman at centre half (and the year before it was Alan Churchard, who went onto being a leading coach in Canada.)

SECONDARY SCHOOL

After junior school came secondary school at age 11 – a move away from the cosiness of the village to South Wigston Boys' High School. I narrowly missed a scholarship to Loughborough Art College, and my exam results were not good enough to get me straight into Guthlaxton Grammar School. No matter.

I excelled in what effectively was a "lower league" academically, being placed in the top class every year, and achieving top pupil in the whole year overall for three straight years.

Sports-wise I was not so good, although I did make the rugby team in the first year after showing suitable aggression in the gym early on. However, in years two and three all the other boys in the team grew, apart from me. So I was dropped. Too small and puny, with little skill at rugby.

The High School was a traditional rugby school of some pedigree; we were not allowed to play soccer on sports day; the Grammar School had both rugby and soccer teams.

Out of school, in games with friends from the village on the local park, I was regarded as a reasonably good player and was usually at least second or third pick for our teams. However, as far as playing for the school team at Guthlaxton was concerned I was nowhere. I simply did not make the squad, even as reserve. Sure, it was a much bigger school, but it really did not make sense.

Then it dawned on me. Even though I did not make the team, I was always a loyal supporter and turned up to cheer on our school team. Then I noticed it. They all wore Terylene trousers – you know, the quality ones that kept their shape even in the rain. Mine, on the other hand, were the cheap wool mix that needed to be ironed every day! Also, on balance, I sensed that their Mams did not work for a living, and that the family were able to exist on the wage of the father.

Ha! They were verging on being middle class! Dads worked in offices rather than factories.

This was quite openly apparent and the sports teachers doubtless took note when it came to team selection. A veritable clique of regular team members emerged, loosely based on class, although I guess the school demographic in this solid Labour Party area was upper-working class at best.

Gosh! My first taste of institutional discrimination, or is it misguided prejudices coming out and that old 'ghost' – the feeling I was a victim of circumstance - coming out? (Refer back to my accounts of junior school to see what I mean.)

In spite of this apparent disadvantage, I seem to recall in my later years at the school my parents *were* able to afford Terylene trousers for me, but by then the die was cast and I never did make the school soccer team.

Just to double the irony, on leaving school, the first soccer team I was invited to join and played for – week-in, week-out – was made up largely of guys from another grammar school who were what I would normally regard as quite posh, and from quite well-off backgrounds. Long live meritocracy! My faith in my abilities was therefore restored, at least on the soccer pitch.

I may have mentioned Dave Freeman earlier. He, together with his Mam, two elder brothers and a sister, lived opposite us in The Avenue, Blaby. Before Melvyn he was my first friend – pre-school - and we "palled out" (as we used to say = became pals) until his creativity – and my relative lack of it – led to a parting of the ways.

His Mam must have been divorced, because I never remember seeing a father. Both of his brothers were talented artists – commercial artists they were called then – before 'graphic designer' took over.

Dave was equally talented. Dave, Mick Charlton, and I were selected to sit a one-day practical art examination at Loughborough Art College. We travelled to the college, some distance away, where I recall we sat to eat "school dinners" served up in a refectory (canteen). This phased me somewhat because I was used to eating sandwiches that I took to school every day at Blaby.

The second thing that made me apprehensive was the prospect of going to a boarding school. I could not even contemplate not going home at the end of school every day to the family home and my Mam and Dad. I failed the entrance exam – which must have been a big relief. Mick failed also, but Dave passed.

I am not sure, but Josephine Shepherd in our class at Blaby Juniors may have also sat the exam and passed. I was always in the top five at school and I think Dave and Josephine – plus Lois (Lulu) Bailey – ranked ahead of me, at fourth, with Mick coming in at fifth.

I saw no more of Dave after age eleven. Ultimately he went to Canada with his family. I would love to connect with him one final time...

He was a big guy even then. Nobody started a fight with him, although another superb pupil and sportsman – Derek (Dec) Pawley often threatened. Nobody was a better fighter than Dec other than that. Thank goodness he was so friendly, naturally pleasant, as well as being an excellent soccer player.

Dave must have been handsome I guess. I say this because, even at eleven, he had a girlfriend, Pat Jones. I remember that she was nuts about Dave. She and her friends used to hang around with us on Blaby Park, principally on account of Dave.

I think I must have *wanted* a girlfriend too. Lulu Bailey was her name, and best friend of Josephine Shepherd. Jo was nice.

Lulu was quite posh whereas I was a tad below her pay grade. I recall that she would never dance with me in country dancing classes. However, another Bailey – Pat, but no relation, did – and she was an excellent dance partner.

That was back in the Junior School days, but now we are ready to go up to 'the big school'.

Here was the deal: the "Leicestershire Plan" was that you all went to a High School from Junior School – at aged 11 years old. The filter as to which class or 'stream' you went into at High School, was the '11-Plus' Exam. Then, after three years at High School you had the option either to stay at High

School for a further two years – before leaving at aged 15 to go to work. There was no exit examination.

Alternatively you could elect to go to a Grammar School at aged 13 where you would be expected to stay until aged 16 or 17 – another three years. You could then take "Ordinary Level" General Certificates of Education ("G.C.E.'s"), after which, if grades were good enough, you took "Advanced Level" G.C.E.'s. You needed A-Levels to get into university.

The other option was to "take articles" in a profession such as a barrister or accountant. Becoming an articled clerk involved your parents paying the law firm or accountants for your training – I think up to 5 years. For the record – the latter was out of the question for me, although one of my best friends – Mick Charlton – took this route. In accountancy.

Anyway, back to the plot. I did well at South Wigston Boys' High School. I narrowly missed going to Grammar School at 11 years old because my '11-plus' exam results were not high enough. (You needed better grades for that.)

I was, however, placed into the top class (or stream) at High School, where I was top of the class every year for three years until leaving to go to the Fourth Year at Guthlaxton Grammar School.

My very good friend, Mick Charlton, also made the top class where he was always in second place, for three years. (My lifelong friend, Melvyn, was two classes below me. Just saying that for reference. Not having a go, Melv! And, for the record, you shouldn't say you were 'thick'. My wife was just reading your last published book of poetry and says that 'you must be very, very clever'. Her words.)

I made the school team in rugby and cricket – but I knew I was an after-thought for the selectors. I was there just to make up the numbers, whereas Mick was a real star at both. A superb athlete. (No sulks on my part, this time. Mick – you were terrific.)

The other transition was at athletics. I usually came 3rd to Dave Freeman's 1st and Derek Pawley's 2nd at the 100 yard sprint. Mick came 4th. This was at Junior School.

At High School Mick could soon out-run me – essential for rugby – and he was an all-rounder at cricket (excellent fast bowler as well as batsman). Conversely I was made full-back at rugby, or was "lost" in the scrum. At cricket I was always last to bat and placed on the boundary when fielding but – most importantly, I was delegated – relegated? - as scorer or 12th-man. "A nobody".

I hated both roles in both sports. I hated being an also-ran. Rugby meant cycling to school in sub-zero temperatures on Saturday morning in mid-winter – to play in freezing cold on a frost-baked hard muddy pitch. Cricket involved staying after school until 6 o'clock in the evening and being late for tea. Both sucked. Even a school trip to Twickenham – I guess to see the England rugby team play, and to Leicester Tigers Rugby - meant very little to me.

(Amazing! The Tigers' ground was in such a sorry state, the wooden stands – the steps – were so rotten through as to be unsafe. Compare that to now.)

The High School was divided into two – one for girls, the other for boys. The only time we were able to mix was at break. For the first two years we tended to keep separate – using free time to play soccer in the playground. The usual – pretty innocent – stuff with girls was a new experience for some of us behind the bike sheds.

In the Third Year, as teenagers, we switched our attention to girls. They were exciting times, although I never formed any attachments – unlike Mick, who "went steady" with Mary Featherby and various of my school friends had girlfriends too – on and off.

About that time I noticed Steve Jarvis and how good he was at sports - at break-time. He was a year below me. It was not until I was 20 years old that we became friends and fellow team members at soccer. Meanwhile – as a 13-year-old – he was going out with a girl I later became totally 'in love' with. To save blushes, I will not name her and I will be the first to admit, *how could it have been love!?*

I never spoke to Steve about this even when – all those years later - we became very close friends. Sadly, he died a few years ago. Our friendship was "disconnected" when I left my home town in 1970 but I was so pleased to meet up with him at a reunion – 47 years later! I still treasure those last moments, heightened by the years of separation.

Ironically, I learnt that he had started to see that same girl again – as a friend – up to quite recently. Yes, again when he was in his sixties – a few years before he died. That said, I still saw him as a dear friend and still do . Even though he won the heart of the girl I had 'loved' as a 16-year-old, I never begrudged him for it. And he never knew.

Only Melv – still best friends since we were six years old – has ever known, even to this day.

I might as well talk about This 'mystery girl' now, to lay it to rest. Romantically I thought of nobody else, pretty much, for eight years. I declared how I felt about her in a brief letter – just the once – that I handed to her one day when she was walking home from school with her sister.

She replied some days later with a similar letter, delivered by hand in similar fashion. Barely any words were exchanged by us at these brief 'deliveries'. I kept her letter with me for some 10 years before I burnt it. In it, she had explained that she could not go out with me and that there were "other fish in the sea". (Her words.)

For years later I suffered in silence. I never contacted or bothered her again. I guess that was to my credit. One hears of so many instances these days when this so-called love leads to "stalking". I never succumbed to that, which I suppose must have also been so *difficult* because she lived a few streets away in the same village.

Not only that, she was clearly "the village beauty" and her name came up many, many times among mutual friends – especially those who were in her class at school. (A year and a half below me.) I can hardly call it a fascination driven by sex. As a hopeless romantic when it came to "the ideal girl" I was fascinated by film-stars such as Sophia Loren, Natalie Wood and Doris Day. Ha! Without knowing why?

All I wanted was to lay down in the tall grass on a warm summer's day, looking up at the shapes of the clouds in a clear blue sky, with the girl of my dreams next to me. Plus my faithful dog, Bess, of course. Barely talking. (That's me and this perfect girl – not me and Bess), doing no more than holding hands. (Again... oh, you get the drift.)

I guess she went to university far away for most of the time for which I was "carrying this torch". But the rejection she handed me when I was a 16-year-old lasting until my early twenties shaped my personality, my moods, my relationships with friends and family – and became a barrier to accepting any other girl as a substitute. It was amazing that I was blessed with so many friends – or indeed had any! Thankfully they tolerated me.

Don't get me wrong – I did manage to have the occasional girlfriend – but they were half-hearted relationships and never went anywhere. Anyway. More of this, later.

I suffered academically at grammar school compared with high school. The 'mystery girl' (I will call her MG) episode was a constant cloud. I performed poorly in class. I was used to being 1st in exams and class work back at the High School, but at Guthlaxton I averaged 13th - half-way down the rankings. Mick (Charlton) over-took me – coming in at 6th or thereabouts. Furthermore, he excelled even more at rugby and cricket. The only saving grace was that I avoided being picked as twelfth man or scorer for the school cricket team or as full-back at rugby.

Also to my advantage, Guthlaxton offered a soccer option – whereas South Wigston Boys' High was purely a rugby school. No soccer. However, I failed to shine in practice and trials so I never made the team.

Things were not looking too bright!

Why were lessons SO difficult? I always had my doubts about my true abilities at High School; I never took my 1st place for granted; but 13th? I was in another league and just could not cut it! Simple.

And all this time the 'MG' shadow haunted me day-by-day, month-in-month-out, during my most important school years. OK, so it wasn't *all* bad. I made new friends in class – different friends from those in the village out of school. So I had two sets of friends – with sport being at the centre of both.

The "girls thing" at school – in general - was something I had to get used to, compared with the all-boys High School. Naturally I gravitated towards, and seemed to get on with OK, those girls who were considered attractive. On the one hand that was fun, but on the other I couldn't shake off my issues with 'MG' and find an actual girlfriend. This did not help when 'MG' – a year below – started at the same grammar school. So near yet ...

So my first kiss came with another girl - when I was 14-year-old and at Jane Thomas' party at her parent's house. Jane was platinum blonde with bright red lips, a bubbly personality, but not one to whom I would ever be attracted. Nor she to me. She was a school-mate, in my class.

Her best friend was Diane Pearson – another blonde – who we all loved as a lovely fun girl, but one who knew how to keep us all at the right distance. She was THE most popular girl and for the right reasons, behaving in the right way to avoid damaging her reputation. Best of all, she never traded on her popularity or looked down on the rest of us, or other girls. We all LIKED her.

I cannot recall *the name* of the girl I first kissed but I do remember that she had a withered leg and a limp – perhaps polio? That said, she was pretty.

How did the kiss come about?

At the party we had "Postman's Knock" where one girl and one boy would be paired at random to go into the under-stairs cupboard. And kiss.

We – this girl and I - only ever did it the one time. We never talked before during or since. Not a word.

The only other aspect I recall from that party – or cycling over to it – were the news reports coming over the radio when I left home about race riots in Little Rock. I had no idea where that was – in the USA – but I had this fear that "they were coming over here". Ridiculous. And why? Strange.

The fellow class-mates I mixed with – boys and girls – gave me an OK social life despite my hang-ups. That said, maybe I should have studied harder IN CLASS and been more disciplined. As a result, my G.C.E. O-Levels were mediocre and I barely qualified for A-Levels in Six Form to become a candidate for university.

The crowd I mixed with in the first term at 6th Form were not doing me any good. I was distracted. We spent a lot of time on what was called the 6th Form Landing – our "territory" - where we did the minimum of A-Level study, and the maximum talking, messing about and playing our guitars.

After three months at A-Level I left without further qualifications at Christmas to look for work. My Dad wanted me to be a barrister, or follow a career in the RAF or police. In the end I landed a job as an insurance clerk with a January 1963 start.

Dad was OK about that because my collar was white, not blue. So...

I NOW WORK FOR A LIVING...

Insurance was considered an "almost" career – a semi-profession. But it was not the same as becoming an accountant or a solicitor or barrister. Or even an officer in the military. The one characteristic that did provide some degree of credibility and status was the presence of ex-military officers in the management. That was then. Things are different now.

For a junior in the midst of this aspiring elite commercial environment it helped me develop some degree of professionalism in terms of bearing, dress and respect for authority and the rules. Looking back, it was so cool to be addressed as '*old boy*' by a retired colonel or ex-RAF officer, and a privilege to be asked to run their errands for cigarettes. (And to be "tipped" with a couple of premium-brand extra long Peter Stuyvesant!)

Unlike modern-day insurance providers which are now based largely on brand-building marketing, companies in the '60's had their roots in tradition and the industrial revolution two centuries earlier. Principally the railways, with the formation of The Railway Passengers Assurance Company, part of the group for who I worked.

You have to imagine a work ethic not based on modern technology – there was no internet – no mobile phone networks – no computer base of any kind. It was all paper, typewriters, phone-based, and face-to-face contact. And personality.

These days email provides immediacy. Then, the equivalent – at least in cities like Leicester – were the four mail collections and deliveries PER DAY. That said, perhaps to save money on postage stamps, one of my tasks was to hand-deliver post to key brokers, legal firms and other insurance companies within the commercial districts.

Looking back now that was funny. I had free licence to 'take a walk' for an hour around the city – or for however long it took – delivering documents and picking up sandwiches for colleagues.

That first year – early 1963 – was 'the big freeze'. Snow hit – in February? - and icy pavements lasted into April! But did I care? Apart from the "why did you take so long, John?" levied at me by the Chief Clerk. Looking back I lacked urgency – and my ability at filing legal papers was slow and so poor.

Life so far had been very much village based but I was not phased by life in the city. Nor was my best friend Melvyn who worked in retail for a national chain of outfitters, and then in manufacturing as a factory manager. We adapted easily.

We met up regularly at lunchtimes. This included a Friday treat now and again at the exotic – for us – Hung Lau Chinese restaurant. It cost four shillings – real extravagance. Twenty pence (cents) at today's money which would be worth about £5.00 today – but we did earn seven pounds (about a hundred and fifty pounds) a week.

Recently I learnt that Hung Lau was run by the father of Gok Wan! If we only knew then...

By this time, we – Melvyn and I – had started to go out at weekends to dances. (There were no discos or clubs as we know them now.) Occasionally – on a Friday – we also went to the Palais de Dance for a lunch-hour of dancing to records. An early version of disco. It cost a shilling. (Five pence)

Of course, our main aim was to meet girls. I still had my hang-up over "you know who" and Melvyn did have casual girlfriends – but he had still to meet "the one".

Now here's a thing – and just to demonstrate what a sad person I was at the time. There was a girl in the typing pool who was pestering me to go out with her. I had no interest whatsoever. Later in the year we re-located offices when we merged with another company, only for me to end up attracting yet another girl who spent most of the day making eyes at me. Two of them. Competing! In one office.

I am not showing off or anything. Really. It's just to explain what a hopeless case I was right then.

The merger brought changes. I took on a more responsible job. We were a much more fun group of work colleagues. However, with that came the requirement to take professional exams or you were out. I tried to study but my heart just wasn't in it. I was bored by the prospect. So I resigned.

But just before I resigned...

I was at a stage of quite enjoying life in Leicester – at least at lunch-hours. As well as Chinese cuisine and mid-day dance hour on Fridays we had a coffee-bar culture just off the clock tower in Leicester.

I had relocated offices and so had Melvyn when he had that career change from retail into manufacturing. We found we were virtually next-door neighbours. We added snooker and darts into our lunch-hour recreation – including a couple of pints of Everard's finest beer – as well as packing into a local coffee-bar where we kept the jukebox fuelled, and ourselves filled, with espresso and toasted teacakes.

(Why was it always a Greek guy that ran them?)

Anyway, it was fun. We all had jobs and enough money to spend. Rock and roll was thriving. We started to play as well as listen to guitars. We were teenagers for goodness sake. What's not to like?

I should say at this point that soccer was a massive part of all this – not just watching Leicester City but also forming and playing for a local team in a local league. Melvyn and I were team-mates, and he had a fine reputation as a Jimmy Greaves-like scorer of goals...

GOODBY INSURANCE... HELLO...?

Disenchanted with insurance as a career path, my plan was to gain two A-Levels and apply for university to read English. Our friend, Phil, was at Newcastle University and I was inspired by his stories of university life.

I signed up for Latin, English and Spanish at A-Level at The Charles Keene College of Further Education for two years, in 1965. But I had to pay fees. There was no grant for this level of study.

The cost of further education was funded by my brother-in-law Derek – my sister's husband and "second Dad" - setting me up as a self-employed window-cleaner. This enabled me to work 20 hours a week and earn as much as I had working full-time in insurance, whilst releasing me for 15 hours attendance at college.

After my initial fear of heights I mastered window-cleaning and earned an excellent hourly rate – necessary, of course, to compensate for bad weather. At least I could use that down-time effectively in study. It was a perfect match – work and study. And play.

I became extremely fit and agile – not an ounce of fat on me. However, I suffered some derogatory remarks from my peers regarding the status of my employment. Being a window cleaner was considered very low grade – worthy only for those who did not have the ability or imagination to do anything else. That said, I was earning more than most of my critics in half the time.

My parents were OK with my career path and being a window cleaner. After all, their son-in-law Derek was making good money as such, and providing a good life for his family as a result. The funny thing was, Derek didn't understand *why* I needed all that education when I could have earned twice as much if I did twice the hours. But I was thinking about a long-term career.

For me, the satisfaction of 'working my way through college' to better myself was enough – and counterbalanced any prejudice against the means by which I was achieving my goals. And because fellow students were also in the 19 to 20 age range I fitted in well. It was not really like going back to school – even though I could have stayed on at school two years earlier for the same qualifications.

It was a nice balance. I was earning and I was learning. With an aim in life. Direction.

I made friends in college and, around about the same time, made new friends out of college but in our village of Blaby. Enter Russ and Ken – who are still friends to this day. Paul was another, but we lost track of him long ago. They were all younger than me and still at grammar school when we first hooked up together.

As it turned out, some of the guys I befriended at college also knew Russ and Ken. Baz Long was one. The others' names escape me.

Boring though it may be to say this, I was still hung up on 'MG' – but I did manage to go out with one or two girls. They were not serious, did not last and – apart from one – did not involve a 'full relationship', if you know what I mean.

Disappointingly, there were really only two girls at college who were worth getting to know (!).

One was just like a fashion model and in my

classes. Slim, attractive, sophisticated and whose background and status was probably above my pay grade. Eventually we went on one date, which was a disaster. She had a friend so I fixed her up with Ken on a blind date to make up the four. Ken is taller than me, but his date towered over even him. Ken hated me for it long afterwards. I never saw the model again socially. What *was* I thinking?

The other girl I will call Susan. It may have actually been her name. (Shame on me, I can't remember.) She had a younger sister who went to school with Ken and Russ.

Throughout the second year until my course ended there was this beautiful girl I would see in the canteen or in the corridor between classes. I think she was studying Commerce. I cannot recall ever actually talking to her whilst we were both actually at college. It was no more than a look or a smile as we passed in the corridor between classes.

Until the end of term.

Back then, the fun part of being in a crowd was piling into someone's car and driving out to some pub in the country – the wonderful East Leicestershire countryside. In summer. I can still smell the scent of new-mown hay.

You 'had to be there', but it was magical. Maybe half a dozen or more car loads descended on one country pub. For the occasion in question it was the end of term get-together for Ken and Russ' year at Guthlaxton Grammar School. It was a warm June or July night – with music and dancing.

I think I must have had a ride out there with Baz Long in his car – a Ford Eight. And one other – I cannot recall his name but I can 'see' him now – he was Polish. When we arrived, after half an hour's drive, or less, imagine my delight when who should be there but "Susan". Her sister was also there, as were Russ and Ken and a whole bunch of others – I guess Elmo (in his open-top Morris Minor!), Wainy, Nick, Johnny Carter – many more.

As the night wore on, with a couple or three pints in me, I asked Susan to dance. She said "yes" and we just kept on dancing together until the pub closed. I simply could not believe my luck. She seemed really 'into me' – an added, unexpected, bonus.

So now I'm thinking, "We are getting on so well. How come I wasted a whole year at college before having the gumption to get to know her properly?"

As luck would have it, she lived not far from Baz Long. Therefore he drove me back home – with Susan and me on the back seat of his car getting to know each other even better. (I won't spell it out for you.)

OK, 'nothing else happened' - before you ask.

But I never saw her again. I may have taken her phone number but somehow we never arranged to meet again. It finished without even starting. To make things worse, my own course had finished so I wasn't returning to college next September.

I tell you now for certain, she would have erased all my issues with 'MG'. She really was something else and I was so clueless – no, *so stupid* – that I never tried to find a way to contact her again – somehow. That's right – *I didn't even try!*

Although I was able to drive, I didn't buy a car until after I left that college. Therefore, I had to ride

4-5 miles carrying my ladder and bucket on my push-bike to do my window-cleaning round. Likewise, it was two bus rides and an hours travelling from home to college, in Leicester. The other side of town.

Kids today simply would *not* stand for it. In those days you just did it.

Unfortunately, my A-Level grades were not good enough for me to take up the provisional places I had reserved at Newcastle University or Warwick. I carried on cleaning windows but I guess I still only averaged 30 hours a week 'earning'.

As you can imagine I didn't mind that. Plus, I was bringing in good money – enough to buy my first car. A VW Beetle with a crash gearbox.

Throughout college I still paid my parents full board for living at home. This was £4.00 a week from a wage of some £10.00 or so. If I earned £10.00 to £12.00 in any week, I would give them sometimes up to double what they expected. They both worked long hours but were not high earners, so I was so pleased to be able to make a substantial improvement to their quality of life. It was great to know they were "more comfortable".

ROLL OVER BEETHOVEN –
SORRY - VOLKSWAGEN!

I learnt to drive with a driving school assisted by my Dad in his Morris Oxford at weekends. On the second test I passed.

That Friday I asked, "Can I borrow the car?"
The answer was, "No."

Forever. It was fine for me to drive it as a learner with Dad in the passenger seat, but not OK for me to take it on my own. I was quite put out. After all, he had let Brian drive it on his own to take his girlfriend out. But Dad was right.

I paid £130 for a ten year old VW. A few weeks later I drove it into a ditch coming back from a pub in The Langtons one night. Luckily there was only minor damage and neither me – nor my passenger, Phil – were hurt. (Phil never rode with me again!)

Having a car meant I was more flexible for work and I could go out at night without having to rely on buses. Just to recap: I failed to get into university so I carried on as a window-cleaner. However, this was only supposed to be a temporary measure whilst I looked for 'a proper job'.

This proved harder than I expected. The problem was that I was not entirely sure *what* I wanted to do for a career. I was inspired by some close friends who worked for companies selling into the grocery trade – biscuits and chocolate - as travelling salesmen. The appeal largely lay in the fact that these jobs came with a new car provided.

I applied for similar jobs but proved a dismal failure at that, too. At interviews I was unconvincing trying to explain why I wanted the job – given that I was obviously quite intelligent with seven O-Levels and two (albeit low-grade) A-Levels. But on the other hand I was happy being a window-cleaner. Apparently. So they said.

It was on one of these trips to an interview in Trowbridge – an hour or so away – that I miss-judged a bend in Corsham and rolled the VW.

It was a write-off.

Whilst my Dad hardly said anything, I dare say he felt he had made the right decision refusing to let me borrow his car.

Even after the accident, I made it by bus from Corsham to Trowbridge for the interview. A few days later I got a letter them – Express Dairies. I was offered a position, but in Coventry, seventeen miles away from where I lived. With no car, and no desire to re-locate, I turned it down. Looking back, I really didn't display much backbone or willingness to leave the comfort of my parents home.

I went without a car for a few months and reverted back to cycling to my window-cleaning round. Although this put me back to a social disadvantage as far as being able to get around, ironically I was getting closer to my first 'full relationship' with a girl.

Well? How else should I phrase it?

One occasion was just before I wrote off my car. I was getting on well with this one girl we used to see at a pub out at Gumley, or some-such village. They had a band at weekends and we – a crowd of us from Blaby plus Wainy from Braunstone - were regulars.

This girl and I arranged to meet up that Thursday to play tennis. That was the last thing on my mind, and I know the last on hers! (Let me explain, this was the era of 'hot pants'! Oh, happy days.) This was Sunday. My interview – and the car crash - took place on Tuesday. As a result I stood her up but quite unintentionally. (I mean come on – *why would I?*)

When we all went out to Gumley the following week I tried to explain all this to her, but she would have none of it. It was a bummer at the time but it may have been shortly afterwards that I had better luck – if that's the right word.

Paul and I were in Leicester having a drink in some pub or other when this real beauty of a blonde girl caught me eye. Petite, nice figure, and quite outgoing. Flirty. She was with three others – two guys and a girl. I just kept looking over – I couldn't help it – until she spoke first. To me. That was it.

I just went over and sat with her, leaving Paul sat on his own with his pint. As it turned out one of the guys was her blind date but she was no way interested in him.

Enter John-Boy...

I must have still been without a car because we had to meet up at the main bus station and so on. We went out a couple or three times during which our attraction progressed to advanced intimacy. (Well, what else should I say? Use your imagination.)

Finally, when my parents were away on their two week summer holiday (so I was 'home alone') we did the deed. In our house. In my bed. That's all I'm going to say about it, mainly because I was rubbish(!), if you really want to know the truth.

Without trying to rationalise too much, I suppose I was looking for more – and we had hardly started to connect other than on a physical basis. What I do remember on the day "it happened" was that, amusingly, my pal Phil knocked on the door to see if I wanted to go to the pub that evening. He was so put out when I said I was busy and that he could not come in. Ha! I closed the door on him without explaining exactly why.

('Go to the pub? You're joking!')

To make it worse, for Phil, Russ was in Wales visiting friends and family at that time, so Phil just had to trudge off to the pub on his own.

No matter. It just seemed funny at the time.

RUSS AND I PLAN A ROAD TRIP

I will fast forward now 3-4 years now – to when I was about 23 years old.

Plenty happened between what I have just covered to when Russ and I left our respective homes to 'migrate' down south to Devon and Cornwall. Basically it was the 'same-old-same-old' repetition and boredom in our social lives that made us get off our backsides and explore a life beyond idyllic Leicestershire.

Up to that time, the highlight of the week was always playing soccer for our local team. For me at any rate. That camaraderie was exceptional. The sense of belonging was unequalled and has never since been equalled but, for me at least, the rest of the week tended to be uninspiring. My life was empty and I was bored – lonely.

Sure, there was a group of us who gathered down the pub at weekends and randomly mid-week. Some of us – but not me – had started to get serious girl-wise and this period was interspersed by the odd wedding (!) - some friends even started families.

Others began making noises about emigrating to

Australia – or Canada, where Ray Churchard's elder brother had gone some years earlier. Looking back I have to laugh at myself when I recall I was so dead against NZ and Australia because reports were that pubs closed before 9.00 pm.

I'm being serious!

Pub life meant so much to me that it was a deal breaker. I went seven nights a week, usually limiting my intake to five pints maximum. Rarely did I 'have too much'. But there was no way I was going there!

After a year of talking about it, Ray and one of the guys, Tony Wainwright (Wainy) went through the process and emigrated to Canada. The fact that Wainy had finished with his girlfriend, Gill, was the tipping point for him. Ray just needed to explore other options in life.

Within our group there was a sub-group as it were – Wainy, Ken and Russ. Russ and I were team-mates as well as pals off the pitch – but he was always with some girl or other, whereas I was, well, you know the rest.

The year before Wainy and Ray emigrated we all went down to St Ives on holiday. Russ, Steve Jarvis (Jarvo) and myself made up the quorum. I don't think Dave Bell went – not sure why. Phil might have started a new life with the BBC in London by then. So he didn't go either. Not sure. Dave Smith was married, as was Melv – and Ken. They *couldn't* come.

I met a girl on that holiday and continued to see her on and off in Liverpool (where she was from) or St Ives (where she worked in a hotel). Not that I could see it immediately, but that relationship was going nowhere so I had no real ties. As for Russ, it must have been that he was "between girlfriends". I don't really know. But the idea of a road trip to the sunny beaches of Cornwall galvanised us over the winter, ending with us both quitting our jobs and setting off in April 1970 in my Wolseley 15/50 topped up with petrol, each with £100 saved.

I guess I need to devote a whole chapter to that experience because it was a game-changer for both of us. It helped me to "grow up" - eventually but finally – and for Russ it was valuable experience as a labourer building roads that laid the foundations for him developing a career in the cement business. (Pun intended.)

For me, it even made the local Leicester Mercury newspaper – sort of! I had simply packed in my window-cleaning round and taken off with no word to any of my customers. One of them in Hartop Road actually wrote to the newspaper to ask if anyone knew where I was!

SO, FINALLY...

Russ and I were on our way – breaking our ties with Blaby and Leicestershire for, eventually, new lives in Devon and Cornwall.

We still live in Devon, individually and with our respective wives, me in South Devon, Russ in North Devon. Over the past 50 years or so we have carved quite different careers and personal lives. But we still keep in touch and will never lose sight of how it all started for us both in 1970.

In many ways, a Golden Year.

To be continued...? For the time being try this 'supplement to the supplement' before our 'trip'.

THE COUNTY ARMS YEARS
No sex, no drugs - just rock n roll
A tribute to an iconic venue not to be forgotten!

In my later teenage years the centre of the universe became The County Arms just outside the village of Blaby – where I was a regular until the end of the 1960s and my early twenties. I would go there at least three nights a week and often more, either with pals or even on my own.

It was the Mecca for live bands - local and some from further afield - so I guess there was plenty of sex and drugs, but it was less obvious then - at least in my circle. Although all of us were as much 'into girls' as you could be, sex wasn't as blatantly shown in the media - TV, Film (there was no internet anyway).

As for drugs, we 'heard about' them - mainly pills within the Mod community - but it didn't become so ingrained into everyday society as it is now, to a level where people's lives and families 'suffered' through drug abuse. Maybe it was becoming more intense within inner cities, but we were yet to see hard drugs like cocaine, heroine and derivatives affecting a broader society – and villages.

Up to this time, marijuana was seen to be

confined to the jazz and beatnik culture – plus American air bases during the war. From the mid-sixties onwards, of course, it became systemic within the hippie culture before migrating into all classes and all sections of society to this day.

That's how it appeared within our circle in any case. It may have had stronger influences and presence in large cities like London, Manchester, Liverpool - and even Birmingham. But not Blaby.

And we certainly did not come across it at The County Arms.

I guess every town in the UK had its equivalent venue at that time, supporting the emerging British talent which was spearheaded by The Beatles from 1962 onwards. The main circuit for UK and American touring artists and bands included the De Montfort Hall in Leicester itself, where I saw The Beatles (twice), the Rolling Stones, The Animals and many other UK acts as well as American stars such as Dion, Del Shannon, Tommy Roe, Chris Montez and so on.

(A few years earlier, in 1958 I think it was, my brother was lucky enough to see Buddy Holly.)

Getting back to a more local level, The County Arms was a major player for live bands, where I saw - or guess I might have also seen - many solo artists who later became world famous. For instance, Ginger Baker and Jack Bruce were in The Graham Bond Organisation - who seemed to feature every 4-5 weeks at The County Arms. As did Zoot Money.

Long John Baldry and The Steam Packet was

another act who I believe, but cannot prove, showcased Rod Stewart and Reg Dwight, alongside Julie Driscoll and Brian Auger and the Trinity.

Most nights at this Everard's Brewery pub they had live music, principally weekends but also Thursday was a 'good night', with (Steve) Fearn's Brass Foundry having a regular slot. Some nights there was a band downstairs and a disco-style dance going on upstairs.

The County Arms was on the main road into Leicester - at Glen Hills - in walking distance from my house, although I drove there when I had a car. The anti 'drink-driving' campaign and the threat of the breathalyser was building momentum but we largely ignored it. So we drank and drove without any guilt or misgivings.

On nights when I wouldn't go along with Russ or Jarvo or any of my other local pals I would be comfortable enough turning up on my own. There were usually a few girls I had soon got to know and I would just spend the evening chatting with them.

I still remember one or two. On Thursdays there was a really nice brunette called Joan with whom I would have a dance or two every Thursday, but she would never go out with me on a date. She was always there with a girlfriend but remained loyal to her regular boyfriend. Even Russ - who was much more attractive to girls than I was - fared no better with her. (Ha! Much to my relief!)

There was another girl - Jean - I used to see on a regular basis and actually went out with her on a proper date - once - before she eventually blew me out because I got too serious. Too 'heavy'. And she wasn't interested. Jeez. I used to get so hung up!

A really special girl who I nearly went out with was called Jill (I think) and lived on Western Drive in Blaby - the council estate. She reminded me of Jean Shrimpton - the No 1 model of the day. One night we were sat talking, just we too, waiting for Graham Bond and the band to start. The patio glass doors leading onto the car park below the dance floor where we were, were immediately behind us, where we sat. Suddenly the doors burst open and what I thought were a couple of ruffians - long hair and scruffy - walked across the floor to the stage. It was set up ready for the band. We were expecting the worst when one of them sat himself down behind the drums and began to play. Loud.

Phew! Not to worry. It turned out to be Ginger Baker! The other was Jack Bruce.

Back to Jill again for one moment, I said I 'nearly' went out with her. True, she did agree to go out with me separate from seeing her at The County Arms but, a couple of days before we were due to meet there was a knock on our front door. I opened it and there she was as pretty us ever, but with bad news.

"I'm sorry," she began," but I can't go out with you." She said no more and to this day, I have no idea why, neither did I say anything - not a word. Apart from perhaps, "OK" as she turned to go and I stood watching her walk away down our drive before I closed the door.

My point is - yes, I was disappointed, but I admired her *so much* for having the decency to say beforehand she wouldn't go out with me, rather than 'stand me up' on the night - which did happen to me a couple of times with other girls.

(You felt a right pillock, having put on your best clothes, got on the bus to town, standing patiently at the clock tower (or wherever you had agreed to meet) at the appointed hour, only to to be still standing there waiting twenty minutes later, after a 'no show'.)

Talking of dress, as I recall, denim jeans were usually out of the question - it was trousers, shoes (no trainers) and a shirt - even a tie and jacket, sometimes, just to go to the pub, and certainly if you went dancing.

One time, to really make an impression, I remember doing something quite ridiculous when I look back on it. The 'Mod' scene was strong and, whilst we were all influenced by it, I cannot class myself as a mod... however.

A really cool guy - a fellow soccer player in Russ's youth team, Mick O'Gleby - came with us one night to The County Arms - sporting a really elegant brown (or was it black?) 'full length leather'. Coat - that is.

It must have been a Thursday because - you guessed it - 'Joan' was there, dancing as usual with her friend. And, also as usual, guys would go up to her, get a dance, only to be blown out after one dance. Then I had an idea - 'this could tip the balance with Joan' I thought. I asked Mick if I could borrow his coat - he said yes, of course - so up I got, put on his 'full length leather', ready to wow Joan with my new outfit - by dancing in it!

'Did it work?' No! 'Did I look a pillock?' Probably. But, hey, you have to try everything. Right?

Earlier I mentioned The Beatles. The second time I saw them they had really 'made it' and (female) fans screamed the place down during live concerts so much you simply couldn't hear them. And that was after queueing from 11pm Saturday night to 10am Sunday morning for tickets, standing on a cold pavement in Leicester City Centre until the booking office opened. It was a waste of time and money.

The first time I saw them it was different.

I treated a local girl from the village to a ticket, buying new jacket, trousers, shirt, tie and shoes to take her out. The performance was all very calm and sedate in comparison, with no screaming fans. The irony was - nearly 60 years later - I received a knock back. I saw a post from the girl in question on a group facebook page and dropped her a note to remind her of our 'date'.

Amazingly - although I have to laugh at myself - *she denied it was me who took her to the show*, claiming she went with her Dad. Now, I know I was always well mannered and respectful on a first date but, to be mistaken for the girl's Dad is a bit rich, don't you think?

It was our only date, though...

At an even more local level, the dances at The Social Centre were not to be missed when they featured live music by 'The Primates', later to be called 'The Foursights'. Dougie Abbot on rhythm guitar, Tim Airey on bass, Dave Lindsey on drums and vocals, and Bill Coleman on lead guitar was the line-up. (It was them who inspired Melv and I to start a group.)

Their covers were excellent, replicating the latest Friday single release by The Beatles on the very next Saturday dance, note perfect. Bill's sister, Bess, was PA to The Beatles at the time, of whom Paul McCartney is reported to have said, "Bess never sold us out."

(A music journalist and true professional, I understand Bess sadly died a few years ago in Australia. She's another who deserves recognition.)

It would appear that The Foursights broke up after a year or two, not sure why, after going to the USA where someone suggested they market themselves as 'The London Knights'.

But Bill went on to play with leading jazz bands, I think Acker Bilk, Chris Barber, and Kenny Ball (but I could have some of that detail wrong) - on double bass - and he still plays every Sunday lunchtime at a pub in Rutland (or, at least, he did until recently).

Other bands who have emerged from Leicester are, of course, Kasabian - but long after The County Arms days. Both Russ and I - but Russ more than me - played soccer with Sergio Pizzorno's Dad, Richard, in Blaby on Northfield Park, and Russ and Richard played for Blaby Boys' Club.

John Deacon of Queen is also an Oadby lad. I think I read somewhere that John's earlier band's first gig was Enderby Town Hall. Ironically, when Melv and I formed the four-piece 'Denhams', that was our first dance at which we played. I think we only had about fifty minutes playlist so, after a ten-minute break, we repeated the first set in the second half! And lived!

A Leicester band that has seemed to have since developed a cult following was 'Legay' - later renamed 'Gypsy'. I remember them as 'Legay' and that they were loud! But the one thing I also recall was that one of the band member's Dads was our bread delivery guy. Mother's Pride. He was SO proud of his boy. Perhaps we should have called it Father's Pride! Ha! I mentioned The County Arms as being on a circuit for emerging acts. Of course, the 'biggy' as a London venue was always Eel Pie Island. 'Gypsy' were on the bill at one of its festivals, way back.

That sort of wraps up the rock and roll scene as far as my personal experience goes, but I couldn't leave the subject without mentioning The Granby Halls and The Il Rondo - the latter an out-and-out Mod hang-out, and where both were favourites with The Who, who I saw live at a Leicester University Rag Week Ball. I remember dancing just feet away from the band on stage – amazing that they played in front of thousands and thousands at Woodstock.

Earlier I mentioned the band that Melv and I started. We lasted about a year, as I recall, but we badly needed a good musician mentor to improve us to survive. We learnt the songs from books of lyrics we bought for nine pence at WH Smiths - there was no online source - no internet - and no YouTube to learn from. As well as musicianship, we lacked equipment - good amplifiers and such. But we played at a few dances and parties - even once at a Leicester University Saturday night dance!

It was another 45 years or so after the break-up before I picked up the guitar to play again seriously. Since 2013 I have made it one of my current daily passions - occasionally playing in our local band - the Teignagers. If only I hadn't packed it in as a true teenager I might have made something of myself.

I left Leicester in 1970 to eventually settle in Devon so, thankfully, I did not witness the decline of The County Arms. Several years afterwards it closed, went into disrepair and, more recently, it has been converted into assisted living for pensioners. Amazing! If I still lived in Leicester I might have seen myself soon ending up in one of those apartments.

But this time armed with a nice collection of guitars and partners for jam sessions!

~ * * * ~

For more details about the author, John Morey, and his published works, visit **NewNovel.co.uk**

Printed in Great Britain
by Amazon